BEHOLD YOUR K____

By Naomi Mitchison

In this enthralling novel, Naomi Mitchison tells the story of the day of the Crucifixion, hour by hour, from the midnight when Peter watched the trial before earliest cock-crow, to the midnight when Mary and James kept watch beside the unmoving stone. The author followed the Gospel story completely, but incorporating some well-established early additions, and making historical sense out of contradictions and difficulties in the light of modern scholarship, especially the new perspectives revealed by the Dead Sea scrolls. All the people affected by that day in Jerusalem appear: the Galilee fishermen, tough and bewildered, the Governor who was not quite a gentleman, the Sadducees playing what they thought were successful power politics with the army of occupation, the dismayed Pharisees, the Roman soldiers discussing the various Gods they have come up against. This is how it might have happened, what they might have thought and said. It is at the same time authentically THEN, but as NOW as though it were happening in London or Calcutta.

Behold Your King

Naomi Mitchison

with an Introduction by
Moira Burgess

Kennedy & Boyd

Kennedy & Boyd
an imprint of
Zeticula
57 St Vincent Crescent
Glasgow
G3 8NQ
Scotland

http://www.kennedyandboyd.co.uk
admin@kennedyandboyd.co.uk

Behold Your King First published in 1957 by Frederick Muller
This edition Copyright © Estate of Naomi Mitchison 2009
Introduction © Moira Burgess 2009

ISBN-13 978 1 84921 031 7
ISBN-10   1 84921 031 4

In memory of my dear friend
LEWIS GIELGUD

Introduction

Naomi Mitchison's novel *Behold Your King*, a fictional treatment of the passion and death of Jesus Christ, was published in 1957. The publisher, Frederick Muller, does not appear elsewhere in Mitchison's lengthy bibliography, and the topic may well seem, to the reader who knows her life and work, equally unexpected. She has described herself as 'a humanist with a strong mistrust of organised religion'[1], and this is the attitude which is most evident in her writing as a whole. As a conventionally brought up child in the early twentieth century, however, she was taken regularly to church[2] and hence she did know the gospel story well. She had already published a novel set in the earliest days of Christianity, *The Blood of the Martyrs* (1938), an allegory of contemporary persecutions in Europe.

Why did Mitchison write *Behold Your King* at this time? She had begun her career with a series of well-received historical novels and short stories set in classical lands and times, for instance *The Conquered* (1923) and *Cloud Cuckoo Land* (1925), and her knowledge of the period is displayed, in passing, in *Behold Your King*: 'There is a certain measure of justice, and even of mercy, in a respectable Roman household' (p. 14); 'the only child his [Greek] parents had been allowed to keep' (p. 15). By the 1950s she had in general moved away from these early themes.

However, the germ of *Behold Your King* is fairly clear, as Mitchison indicates in her foreword:

> The other important sources [apart from the Gospels] are, of course, the Dead Sea Scrolls, in so far as they have been found and read up to 1956. (p. ix)

The discovery of these fragmentary documents, including texts from the Hebrew Bible, in 1947-56 in caves at Qumran near the shores of the Dead Sea, aroused world-wide interest, and the

i

original book jacket of *Behold Your King* is designed to suggest a scrap of Hebrew text.

The blurb in the 1957 edition (which reads very much as if it is written by the author), and the foreword again, provide further information.

> The author followed the Gospel story completely, but incorporating some well-established early additions, and making historical sense out of contradictions and difficulties in the light of modern scholarship, especially the new perspectives revealed by the Dead Sea Scrolls. (half-title page, from 1957 edition)

> Among many modern books, the one to which I owe, perhaps, most is Hugh Schonfield's *Jesus: a Biography;*[3] but I am also indebted to his other books, including his new translation of the New Testament, as well as to his help and advice.(p. ix)

These passages may usefully be read together, for the 'early additions' are certainly (she mentions them again in the foreword) the apocryphal or non-canonical gospels, some fragmentary and some lost but quoted elsewhere (*The Book of James*, *The Gospel of the Hebrews*, and others), on which Schonfield draws. Whether Mitchison read the actual texts or received them as mediated by Schonfield is probably unimportant. What is significant is that they supplied her with certain hints and episodes not in the canonical gospels, of the sort which are a gift to the novelist, such as the attempted rescue of Jesus, the vow of James and the traditional forename of Barabbas.

In addition to all this, letters in the National Library of Scotland – or at least their covering docket in Mitchison's hand – show that she was writing *Behold Your King* during a visit to Jerusalem in March 1956.[4] Though the letters themselves are not greatly informative on the process of creation ('[I am] getting on a bit with my book', she writes), the wild flowers she notices ('masses of scarlet anemone ... a very handsome yellow genista ...') can perhaps be detected in the novel: 'bunches of tulips and field flowers, scarlet and yellow' (p. 112).

Mitchison is far from the only novelist to tackle 'the historical Jesus' or the other characters in the gospel story in fictional form, but many of the familiar titles in this genre were published some years after *Behold Your King*. Nikos Kazantzakis' *The Last Temptation*, for instance, was not published in English until 1961, and Michèle Roberts' feminist treatment of Mary Magdalene, *The Wild Girl*, appeared in 1984. To a large extent – not unusually in her career – Mitchison was ploughing her own furrow.

She may have known Dorothy L. Sayers' play cycle *The Man Born to be King*, broadcast on BBC radio in 1941-2 and published by Gollancz in 1943. Sayers (who was, unlike Mitchison, a committed Christian) gives her characters colloquial dialogue throughout, causing some controversy, much of the protest occurring before the protestors had ever heard the plays. But Mitchison had always used colloquial language in her historical novels: 'I was the first to see that one could write historical novels in a modern idiom: in fact it was the only way I could write them.'[5] Beyond this, it is tempting to wonder if she had read Jorge Luis Borges' short story (or 'christological fantasy', as Borges calls it) 'Three Versions of Judas' (1944), available in English by the late 1940s, which posits the treachery of Judas as a predestined act.[6] Mitchison suggests this in Behold Your King (p. 49).

Armed with such information, inspiration and local colour, Mitchison writes a very fine novel. The structure is strictly defined: twenty-four chapters cover the twenty-four hours of the day which Christians call Good Friday, the day of the crucifixion of Jesus, one hour to each chapter. Some of Mitchison's best work is thus formally constrained: both *Men and Herring* (1949) and *Lobsters on the Agenda* (1952) cover the events of one week, while the foreground action of *The Bull Calves* (1947) is confined to two days and one location, though skilfully used flashbacks expand the scope and vision of the novel.

A novelist retelling the events of Good Friday hour by hour encounters one major technical difficulty. From 3 pm, the traditional moment of the death of Jesus, nothing happens, apart from the laying of the body in the tomb. (Mitchison, a strongly visual writer, would surely have approved, if she knew of it, the symbolism by which a Catholic church is considered to be empty from that hour until Easter Sunday: the sacrament removed from the altar, no music, all images hidden in purple shrouds.) But Mitchison makes effective and powerful use of this – literally – dead time. She shows, firstly, life going on in Jerusalem – Pilate relaxing at a cock-fight, the soldiers gossiping about girls – and, secondly, the followers of Jesus lost and bewildered, all those hopes and promises suddenly in ruin.

The twenty-four hour structure makes further demands on the novelist. The text has to contain a good deal of back story and exposition: who people are, and why the situation has reached crisis point. Mitchison handles this well. The back story is generally conveyed through a character's thoughts, and the viewpoint shifts deftly from one character to another: a Roman, a Pharisee, a follower of Jesus. Occasionally it draws back into authorial comment, and even less frequently (see pp. 48-9, 72, 80, 117-8) the viewpoint is that of Jesus: a daring enough move, which Mitchison accomplishes with confidence and sensitivity.

It is by the characters, of course, that a novel stands or falls, and here Mitchison shows great skill in detaching these historical or (more often) legendary figures from their usual haloed background. Jesus is seen by Pilate and Herod as an unimpressive, uncooperative nuisance of a prisoner. His followers recall an energy in explanation, and a kind of bafflement when they fail to understand. Mitchison as a feminist does not fail to note his view of women: 'every woman was a sister, whose hand he could take' (p. 22), and as a socialist, the inclusiveness of his coming kingdom: 'the slave with his master … all equal together' (pp. 58-9). Can she have known the Woody Guthrie song 'Jesus Christ', dating from about 1940?

> This song was written in New York City
> Of rich man, preacher, and slave;
> But if Jesus was to preach like he preached in Galilee
> They would lay Jesus Christ in his grave.[7]

The disciples Peter, James and John, fishermen from Galilee, are referred to by the nicknames Rocky, Stormy and Flash, 'following the custom of fishing villages all the world over' (foreword, p. ix), and of course the custom of Mitchison's own village of Carradale. Perhaps the sobriquets here have a slightly contrived air – the best nicknames, like the best football chants, somehow arise more spontaneously than this – but the name Flash for John son of Zebedee does serve to distinguish him from another disciple with a major part to play, here called John Priest. There is some debate about the identity of the various Johns in the gospel story, but Mitchison as a novelist must make a decision, and her character John Priest is the disciple 'whom Jesus loved' (John 13:23, 19:26), probably the author of the fourth gospel. Rocky – Peter – is, as tradition seems to indicate, a big lumbering fisherman, physically strong, mentally none too bright, blindly loyal, tortured by his denial at cockcrow. Mitchison read much Kipling as a child[8] and very likely knew the story 'The Church that was at Antioch'.[9] Its Peter and hers are not dissimilar, great slow figures who are yet miracle workers, enabled by a power they hardly understand.

Any confusion about Johns is nothing to the potential confusion of Marys in the gospels and in tradition. Marina Warner has succinctly described the situation as 'a muddle of Marys'.[10] It is unnecessary here to enumerate all the possible permutations of Marys, since Mitchison, again, has taken a novelist's licence to delineate her characters clearly. She has just the two Marys, 'old Mary', the mother of Jesus, and 'young Mary', Mary Magdalene.

Mitchison's portrayal of Mary the mother of Jesus is entirely her own. She does not follow Schonfield, whose Mary is 'somewhat domineering … rather fussy', a stereotypical Jewish mother in fact, with no understanding of her son.[11] Neither does she follow the tradition that Mary spent her early youth as a temple maiden, with the demure and submissive character that implies. Instead other characters remember her:

> … this woman who had been so violent a patriot, so beautiful in her country way … who had been so certain that it would be her own, eldest son who would save Israel. (p. 29)

A beautiful, strange girl who made up songs ... Was it her grandfather who was out with the rebels in old Herod's time? (p. 48)

Incidentally, Mitchison's Mary is not 'ever virgin', as she is described in orthodox prayers and hymns. There is no room here to detail the various theories by which, over many years, James, Joses, Simon and Judas, the brothers of Jesus (Matthew 13:55), have been deemed to be no more than stepbrothers or cousins. If Mitchison knows these, she ignores them, and her Mary is mother of a large family. It is all completely iconoclastic – not a surprise with Mitchison – but it makes sense. Mitchison has looked at the Mary figure so central in Christian tradition and iconography, and decided that – like many of the central characters in her other novels – this must be a strong, idealistic, fulfilled woman.

She is equally definite about Mary Magdalene, around whom so many legends have accrued. She makes her view clear in the foreword:

There is no reason to suppose that Mary of Magdala was the same person as the harlot with whom she is so often equated. I have therefore broken with the romantic tradition over this. (p. ix)

Neither is Mary of Magdala – which is all that Magdalene means – to be identified with Mary of Bethany, the sister of Lazarus, as some of these romances propose. (One can almost hear the practical Mitchison asking 'How could she be?', since Magdala and Bethany are two different villages many miles apart.) Following the gospel, she is, however, the unfortunate from whom Jesus has cast out seven devils (Mark 16:9); that is, in Mitchison's realistic terms, she has had psychotic episodes all her life, and Jesus has cured her. Now she is a kind of groupie, travelling with the disciples, hopelessly in love with Jesus, virginal and shy. After she witnesses the crucifixion her psychosis returns, and the disciples assume she can never be cured now, since Jesus is gone. But Rocky – Peter – cures her, drawing on a power he did not know he had. Thus, in Mitchison's version, Mary Magdalene is absolutely central to the story of Christianity, since it is her healing by Peter which shows the disciples that the spirit of Jesus is still with them, and that they can carry on his work.

This brings us to the main difference between Mitchison's novel and her source Schonfield, and the main surprise for the reader who has taken Mitchison at her own valuation as a humanist. Schonfield writes 'a biography' – the subtitle of his book – of the historical Jesus, and that is the person he portrays, a historical character, a man. Mitchison follows this to some extent, and the other characters – the disciples, the women, certainly Pilate, Herod and the Roman soldiers – view Jesus as a man, whether as an agitator or as possibly the long-awaited leader for Israel. But here and there, throughout the novel, people – from the confused Rocky to the implacable enemy Caiaphas – are allowed by Mitchison to wonder 'What if ...?' And she delicately points up what she is doing by references to other gods: Adonis, Baal, Mithras. It is an extraordinary subtext to what is to all appearances one more novel depicting the historical Jesus. I have argued elsewhere[12] that – ever broad-minded, fair and ready to hear the other side – Mitchison half-believed throughout her life that there might be something, whether a mother goddess, an animistic spirit or the devil, out there. Certainly she allows for that possibility in *Behold Your King*.

Mitchison has never written anything better than the final sentences of this novel, carefully designed so that the reader can choose an ending according to his or her belief, or lack of belief. It is midnight on the day of the crucifixion, and under the full moon of Passover the followers of Jesus are standing around his rock-cut tomb, its entrance blocked by a great stone. What happened next?

Believers say that on Easter Sunday the stone was found to be rolled away and the body had gone: what Christians call the resurrection of Jesus had occurred. Non-believers maintain that the disciples only said this had happened; it was a confidence trick designed to kick-start their mission of spreading the word.

Of course *Behold Your King* does not go as far as Easter Sunday, and this is how it ends.

> There should be an answer. [John] did not know it yet. He looked instead at the great stone in front of the tomb that he had found so heavy. … Gradually they were all looking. The moonlight shone on it very coldly and distinctly, the stone between them and him. (p. 183)

Mitchison, the humanist, the freethinker, is apparently leaving it entirely up to us. But the reader has to absorb not only the words but the sound, the music, of a piece of writing; has to understand what the writer has stated, but also what she implies. In these lucid, simple, beautiful sentences, does Mitchison seem to be preparing us for a confidence trick, or for something – whatever it is – out there?

Moira Burgess
2009

Notes

1 Naomi Mitchison, 'By his works' [review of A.N. Wilson's biography of Hilaire Belloc], *New Statesman*, v. 107, 4 May 1984, pp. 24-5 (24).

2 See for instance NM, 'Perthshire Sabbath,' *Scottish Field*, v. 107, April 1960, pp. 39-40.

3 Hugh Schonfield, *Jesus: a biography* (Banner Books, 1939)

4 National Library of Scotland Naomi Mitchison archive, Acc. 4549/4.

5 NM, *You May Well Ask* (Gollancz, 1979), pp. 163-4.

6 I am indebted to Dr Kirsten Stirling for this suggestion, and for others during the writing of this piece.

7 Woody Guthrie, 'Jesus Christ', c. 1940. This is the last stanza; slightly different versions exist. See *Woody Guthrie Folk Songs*, ed. Pete Seeger (New York, 1973), p. 12. I am indebted to Peter Stirling for this suggestion, and for reminding me, passim, of the atheist's viewpoint.

8 See NM, *All Change Here* ((Bodley Head, 1975), p. 36.

9 Rudyard Kipling, 'The Church that was at Antioch', in *Collected Stories*, ed. Robert Gottlieb (Everyman's Library, 1994), pp. 869-88.

10 Marina Warner, *Alone of All Her Sex* (Vintage, 2000), pp. 344-5.

11 Schonfield, pp. 48, 74-5.

12 See Moira Burgess, *Mitchison's Ghosts* (Glasgow: Humming Earth, 2008).

Foreword

THIS book is based primarily on the four Gospels, secondarily on other early material, some of which has been lost, accidentally or deliberately, but is referred to elsewhere. This includes the story of the attempted rescue and James's vow. The other important sources are, of course, the Dead Sea Scrolls, in so far as they have been found and read up to 1956. Among many modern books, the one to which I owe, perhaps, most is Hugh Schonfield's *Jesus: a Biography*; but I am also indebted to his other books, including his new translation of the New Testament, as well as to his help and advice.

There are a few other points. The question of names is difficult when we come to people whom we know by completely Anglicised names which are very far from their Jewish originals. I have compromised, but have, for instance, kept the completely westernised "James", "John" and "Mary". I have used nicknames for the Galilean fishermen, following not only the custom of fishing villages all the world over, but also the clear indications in the Gospels. Simon bar Jonas was nicknamed Peter, which means Rock; presumably the nearest translation is Rocky. The "Sons of Thunder" (or "of the Storm") were presumably called something like Stormy and Flash.

There is no reason to suppose that Mary of Magdala was the same person as the harlot with whom she is so often equated. I have therefore broken with the romantic tradition over this. I have kept the traditional but quite unauthenticated name of Pilate's wife.

N.M.

One

THE other one spoke to the woman at the great door and slipped something into her hand. Then he went through to the porch that was built, Greek fashion, with pillars, well above the street, and called in a whisper: "Rocky!" Very calm he seemed, his lips thin, his eyes narrow so that nobody could tell what he might be thinking. But Rocky wasn't like that. He couldn't hide what was in him. Never had been able to. They'd see. They'd know. He was deadly afraid to move, even.

The other beckoned with his head, urgently, so that Rocky had to move. It would have been different in some other danger. A wind tearing down off the hills, catching and twisting the boat, smashing her mast. If only he was in his boat now! With something he knew to fight against, something he'd always known, had grown up with, not all these rich city folk and the great house of the priest towering over him, making nonsense of the Kingdom.

But, if he wasn't going on with it, why had he come? Why hadn't he run with the others? Stormy and Flash, they'd both run. Not old Rocky. Old Rocky had stuck to the Son. Always would. He took a breath and pushed through between the city-smelling folk to the door. A grand big door it was, with great bronze hinges spreading into peacocks' tails, and the wood carved all over with signs and letters. Rocky isn't afraid of signs and letters, he said to himself. No, Rocky isn't afraid.

In the courtyard of the house there were more folk. They were saying things—but the other one squeezed his arm hard to stop him speaking. Right enough, if he'd let out with his big mouth and his Galilean tongue in it!

There were torches here and there, stuck high on the walls. Underfoot it was stone with marble pavements running across it, and marble round the well in the corner. In these great houses they'd a well all to themselves, no running to the corner like ordinary folks. And this was the kind of house John Priest knew his way about. Funny; he'd known about it, and yet he'd always thought of John as one of themselves up to now.

Rocky stood there in the dark, looking hard at John, whom they had nicknamed John Priest because he had been born into the priesthood, wondering if he was all right. It had been said that he was some kind of far-out cousin of this Annas. He hadn't thought about it. Now he'd got to. Anything might be true, anything, after seeing Judas coming up with the soldiers. He couldn't somehow believe that, not yet, in spite of what his eyes had seen. But it began to get into his head that anybody might be an enemy. He began to think of that sword. First of all the Son had said they'd need swords, and then, when it was dripping blood in his hand, there'd been this other thing said. If you use the sword, you die by the sword. Much he cared about that now!

It was cold. There, someone was lighting a fire to keep them warm, lighting it on stone, not on the good marble of the pavements. Yes, that was sense; fire would spoil it. And beyond the fire? Yes. Yes. That must be the hall of judgment. The great hall of the great house and jammed with Temple guards. He was somewhere in there, trapped, tied up like a beast for slaughter, in spite of Rocky and his sword. Was this the end of the Kingdom—all a mistake, the net shot wrong? He cast his mind back, only a few days ago. The Son riding in like a proper King, all fulfilled as the prophet Zacharias had known long ago. And the Jerusalem folk and all the pilgrims crying out Hosanna and homage, knowing he was the King. They had gone up from Bethany and there had been the first sight of the Temple, again and always as exciting as the sound of trumpets blown all together, the walls leaping up from the sheer rock, a glitter of gold and marble, old Herod's doing. And that seemed to be their own!

But what had the Son thought about it? Rocky didn't, somehow, know that. You loved the Son, you loved him with a terrible kind of protecting love; the way Rocky had loved his wife when she was a young lass. But he didn't want to be protected. Sometimes he seemed to want terribly not to be protected but to be understood. And you couldn't do that. You were afraid; there was something that shut you out. He was frightening. Sometimes you couldn't bear to be with him. And yet you couldn't bear not to be. It was like that coming down the Mount of Olives among the tossing of the grey leaves. The Son had looked straight ahead of him, not at his own friends all so happy. There was something he had known then and couldn't explain.

Maybe, thought Rocky, looking over to where John stood, sad and young as the leap of the fire lighted and shadowed him, there were those that could understand. They could see through the stories the Son kept telling, see right to the bottom. The clever ones did that. The kind he didn't care for!

So all that time while they were shouting and waving branches and throwing flowers and marching along like an army with banners, on to Jerusalem, there had been this sadness and strangeness on the Son. He, Rocky, he had tried to chase it away. Far be it from you, Master, he had said! This sacrifice, this blood that the Son had spoken about. And now—now it seemed to have come true.

You couldn't see what was going on in there. Only now and then there was a kind of a nasty noise and movement, like the wriggling backs of vultures down over a kill. Rocky pulled at the sleeve of the other one, who leant over so that he could whisper: "Who's that going in, John?" It had been someone important; the guards had saluted and made way.

John whispered back: "That's another of Annas's nephews. It's packed."

"Packed? Against *him*?"

"Yes. Oh, can't you understand—yet?"

"Then they'll . . ."

"Yes." John wiped his face across with the edge of his coat. Was he crying? Rocky couldn't see. Or sweating, in spite of the cold?

John Priest moved away a bit, into completer darkness. Rocky'd been the only one of the Galileans who'd had the guts to follow to the end. But John didn't want to have to explain to him. John knew about what was happening, saw through it in a rational way; he had, after all, been the one to see it coming, except that he had always thought something would happen to stop it. He had been brought up in the party of the Sadducees, the compromisers; he still had plenty of friends there. He had thought, yes, he had been stupid enough to think, that they would be convinced, as he had been, once they had been shown the Way. No, they were immune to conviction. And now he could see how they had it all thought out. They were, essentially, the people of property, the solid core of the nation. They saw themselves as the rightful rulers, but they knew they had to keep on terms with the Romans, had to appear to play their game. They needed to get rid of the Son; he was a danger to their kind, most of all now that he had the pilgrims at his back, and half the Jerusalem mob. Had that been wise, all the same? But it was bound to come, above all since Bethany. If once you start raising the dead, well then, you must be dangerous. People will believe in you even if you are against the powers of the world.

That, in the end, was what the Sadducees couldn't stick. That was what was driving Caiaphas. Jesus the Nazarene could be allowed to preach so long as he did it so that most people didn't understand. He could be allowed to cure and cast out devils; others did that. But when it came to starting riots in the Temple, and raising the dead, it had to be stopped. It was then that Caiaphas decided.

Had the Romans even noticed? John didn't know. They didn't come into the picture directly. It wasn't as if the Sadducee party actually liked the Romans. He wouldn't say that of them; after all, they were Jews. They had reacted decently as Jews when the Romans under this new Procurator took the Corban, their own dedicated treasure, to build filthy Roman sewers! You can't like Romans. Greeks, yes, perhaps. Up to a point, anyway. Can you ever forgive a Roman? I don't know, he thought; I should have asked, and now it is too late. But forgiveness—that, surely, is for someone you can touch a little, someone who might, forgiven, become part of the Kingdom, a brother. It was thinkable to forgive Annas and Caiaphas. But not a Roman. They were on the other side of Cæsar's wall; they would not even go to the same hell as the wicked at this side.

Yet it was Annas and Caiaphas who were doing this thing. If they could convict him and murder him for some crime that would really shock people, they would. Sorcery, perhaps. As though *he* had ever even condoned the dark powers! But if they could not catch him in that trap, they would do it through the Romans. They would put the blame for it on the Procurator, this Pontius Pilate, so that if there was to be a come-back, it would be against him. Clever.

And the Pharisees, the pious, couldn't they see what was happening? Surely they weren't still angry because he had broken some of the rules, the ones that needed breaking? Surely they of all people could see—the Messiah, the chosen one, when he was among them at last? But, as that name came at him, John suddenly ceased altogether from his rational thinking; he flooded, he drowned in knowledge of the hideous, hopeless wrong that was being done in there and he himself powerless to do anything to stop it.

He looked round, finding himself shivering from head to foot; the moon was up now, the cold full moon of the

Passover. Rocky had gone over to the fire to warm his hands and feet. He'd better watch out, John thought, or he'll be recognised. Hasn't he any sense? It was queer, he was fond of Rocky and all that crowd of decent, warm-hearted, quick-tempered Galileans, but now he didn't really care what happened to them. There was only the one love; and that fatal. He had to see.

He moved nearer the hall. Someone was standing on the kerb of the well, holding on to the light, graceful pillar of the cupola. "Nothing to see," said the man; "he won't speak now, the bastard." He jumped down and John took his place quietly, not answering, except with a surge of blood. From up there you could see over the heads of the guards, right into the hall. It was only, of course, the hall of the great house; it had no sanctity, no great age. In fact, it scarcely had the look of a Jewish building; those who had designed and built it had been Hellenisers. Yet there were the priests, nothing but priests in full robes, crowded, sitting or standing. Anyone who didn't know might have taken it for a full meeting of the Sanhedrin, held here instead of in the council chamber by the Temple. But someone who did know would have seen who was and, still more essentially, who was not in this particular gathering. There were hardly any of the Pharisee group, none of those who carried weight such as Nicodemus, Joseph of Arimathæa, nor the older generation of the learned and pious who had no love of politics. Here and there were groups in shadow or faces John did not recognise, but it seemed to him that they were all of one party, and would all side with the High Priest, whatever the prisoner said or did.

·   ·   ·   ·   ·

The prisoner was chained lightly. It had been obvious that he wasn't going to be violent. The first part of the questioning was over. It had been reasonable enough; that is, if the authority of this court was to be recognised at all.

If, for instance, you did not know that it had been called together in order to wipe out this particular prisoner; legally, no doubt, but finally, as a thumb crushes out a fly and it is no more. If this court were in any sense a real court of priests, the High Priest would have a certain right to ask this preacher about his doctrines and about his disciples. He would have a certain right to find out, through witnesses, if the man was practising sorcery, in which case he must, according to the law, die. He might have expected some fear and respect from a country fellow or indeed from any Jew. But this prisoner was showing no fear and no respect. He said quite lightly and casually that he had been preaching and teaching openly, and they had better ask the ones who had taken it in. That had annoyed the officers; one of them had hit him with his staff of office, saying he mustn't speak like that to the High Priest, but it made no difference to the way this prisoner spoke and looked.

Then there had been a question of finding witnesses to prove the sorcery and prove it so as to shock and confound the man's friends and followers. That was meant to have been laid on, but somehow it was not working out. There were plenty of witnesses, and they had been well coached and paid, but what they said didn't make sense. Or rather, it made too much sense. When it came to the point they found themselves repeating what the prisoner had actually said. And that—well, that could not be made to sound evil: nothing he could be condemned for. Yes, there was this about him saying he could destroy the Temple and build another within three days. But the way he said it—you couldn't pretend he was invoking devils or was even a danger to the public peace! Yes, he had attacked the stall-holders who had been carrying on their lawful business in the courtyard of the Temple, upset the stalls and knocked the money about, let loose the sacrificial beasts and generally made trouble for those whose legitimate business was there. But that was not serious enough for what this court wanted.

They asked him what he had to say about it; he smiled and looked at them, and again when the witnesses were called he did the same. He seemed to be refusing even to look like a sorcerer! It was being more difficult than they'd meant it to be. And there was this feeling about: suppose, suppose that after all there was something in it? But the strong-minded did not let that creep in; Caiaphas was strong-minded. He knew that if they let him go now and he went back to his friends and this following that seemed to be growing, the thing would build up out of all bounds. Sooner or later the Procurator would realise, and then he, with all the weight of the Roman power, would clamp down and Israel would lose the freedom it still had when it could be thought of as a law-abiding, solvent province. And the last state of Israel would be worse than the first. So, for the sake of Israel, and for the sake of the ancient priesthood of Israel, this danger spot must go. Yes, thought Caiaphas; in a sense he may be innocent, but he must die for the sake of all of us.

.   .   .   .   .

It was long past midnight now. In the rest of the city men and women were sleeping. Most had eaten the Passover supper that evening, although in some households, where Passover was thought of as a public sacrifice overriding even the Sabbath, it would be kept on the Friday, the Sabbath evening itself. That was so for the Sadducees, some of whom were even Roman citizens; they took the view that it was a matter for the whole State. But for all it was deeply important. Poor families who ate little meat from one year's end to the next, but lived mostly on salt fish and beans and such, would still manage somehow to find themselves the lamb of sacrifice. Country cousins would bring one in, and the wine and the bitter herbs, the almonds, raisins and dates, would be come by one way and another, and all would crowd together for the washing, the eating of unleavened bread, the drinking of the prescribed cups and the singing of the psalms. And once again there would be the sense that the special alliance between Israel and God had been marked and made sure and would endure.

The Romans knew about this. They knew that their subjects would have a special feeling of security and boldness, perhaps even insolence, at this time. Better, though, to let it be. The Sadducee party, ruling under leave of Rome, would realise that feelings were one thing, actions another. So long as this was clear, religions were not really dangerous to administration.

The Temple guards would keep Passover the next evening. So would the priests. Already it was deeply in their minds. Old Annas had been thinking back over many Passovers in many years: bad years, some of them, years of fear and horror, the years of the last madness of the great and terrible Herod when torture and murder were as common for the rich as for the poor; the riots after Herod's son had ordered the troops to disperse the pilgrims. Hardly a family without its dead, at least among the poor. Better to have a house and a door to bar. Those riots had been the fault of the pilgrims coming in, and the worst of them had been Galileans. Never trust a Galilean, Annas said to himself. Nor yet this mob of pilgrims. It was not as if they brought much to the Temple: faith perhaps, but of the crudest kind, likely to develop into revolting superstition and even paganism: rude pawing at the Mysteries, roughness and violence. Like this new Galilean Jesus with his extremism, his violent preaching and refusal to argue reasonably. It had amused some. But he, Annas, he was not amused.

.   .   .   .   .

The night was getting colder. It could be cold out on the nets after nightfall, but not the keen cold of this hill city. Mostly Rocky never noticed such things. But it is cold waiting and keeping quiet. He could see the other one standing on the kerb of the well watching. All very well for him,

2—BYK

Jerusalem born, knowing this house and all. Only so few hours ago, and they had been keeping Passover. He'd got to remember what the Son had said, all of it if he could. It was all mixed up in his mind now with the story of the old deliverance from the power of Egypt. But, when he was breaking the bread, why had he said that it was his body? And the third cup, why had he told them it was his blood? I can't see through it yet, thought Rocky, but I will, I know I will. It was he himself who called me Rocky, half in fun, but half because he believed in me, knew I'd stand true. But in spite of that, he went and said I was going to deny him. He said that when I came barging in, shooting out my neck, saying I'd die for him. And I would so die, right enough! But maybe he wanted to put me in my place, and that's a fair do; always speaking out of turn, that's me. But I'm going to remember, I'm going to think right through it, right down to the very bottom, Lord help me to do that, and then I'll be fit to die for him. But give me time, because I'm not as quick in the wits as some.

There was one of the maids, a sensible woman. She had been about quite a bit in Jerusalem and was one for noticing things. Once or twice she had listened to the new preacher; a new preacher was always worth stopping for. After all, you never knew. But this one—he seemed to be talking in riddles. A crowd of Galileans with him, tough-looking customers. She crossed the courtyard close to the fire: that chap standing there, up from the country, yes, but surely— "You were with this Jesus of Nazareth!" she said. But of course he wasn't going to admit it. "I don't know what you're talking about!" he said. Oh well, maybe she'd got him wrong. But one has to be careful, these days.

.   .   .   .   .

In the hall of judgment the trial went on. The witnesses had been called, and had made a mess of things. And one witness they wanted hadn't been found: Judas the son of

Simon the Zealot. But he might have said something out of turn too: an unstable type, lost his nerve perhaps. Caiaphas wondered what he'd had in his mind when he came to them, as scared as a lost dog, asking for money to betray his leader. There had been a moment when Caiaphas had wondered if it had been a double-cross of some kind, if the man had really been carrying out instructions, anyway doing what this leader of his had wanted him to do. Suppose, for instance, this Jesus had intended to get himself arrested so as to make a public statement. If he was fool enough to trust that the Jerusalem mob would have the guts to rescue him! You never knew what went on in the minds of these extremists, especially the Galileans with all those generations of rebellion behind them. He couldn't have known he was going to certain death.

Or could he? Caiaphas looked at his quiet prisoner. No, he wasn't frightened. Death perhaps didn't mean much to him. Many have died for what they believed in, and most of all those of Israel who are in this special relation with God. As he, Caiaphas, would for certain know himself to be in the coming evening at his own Passover supper, among the lights and the music, the singing of the Hallel psalms. The Passover lamb was sacrificed for them all, and if a man chose for himself to be the sacrifice—he would not follow up that thought. It might lead him farther than he intended. Essentially, this trial was a matter of power. How, then, to shift the power so that it would remain for certain in his own hands?

He leant over and whispered to Annas, who nodded. The sorcery charge must be dropped. At once and completely. It hadn't worked. But now that they had him in their hands, they must carry the thing through. If once they let him go—no, never! There was another charge. If he could be got to give a straight answer. Think, quickly, how to get that.

All right. He knew. He stood up, gathering the priests to right and left, with his eyes and a small gesture of the hands.

"I adjure you," he said, "by the Living God," and he felt the shiver beginning to go round. "Tell us, are you the Christ, the son of God?" Now: if he answers that.

"Yes," said the prisoner.

They all heard him say it. They heard him go on: "And after this you shall see the Son of Man sitting on the right hand of power and coming in the clouds of heaven." Caiaphas looked round, catching the eye first of his father-in-law, then of one of his brothers-in-law who had also been High Priest; in all of them was a tremendous sense of relief. The man had admitted it, had allowed himself at last to be caught. Because he was very tired, or—on purpose? Whether tired or not, he hadn't foxed, hadn't for once answered in riddles. Instead he had answered quite simply and without equivocation, with the kind of assurance someone might have had if—if it could have been true. And for one moment Caiaphas had the appalling notion that after all the thing might be a fact. This might be the Messiah. Then common sense reasserted itself. A Galilean carpenter, a crazy preacher leading the people astray into dangers he couldn't even see. No! That was the fact. Anything else was nonsense.

"You hear," said Caiaphas quietly, to his intent listeners, "he has claimed to be the Christ, the anointed one, the ruler of Israel. This is directly aimed against Cæsar, who is our sole ruler. We are, as Cæsar's friends and keepers of the peace under his authority, compelled to give him up to the Roman authorities, for whatever punishment they see fit to give."

"Death," said Annas, "for what he has said is blasphemy. He has condemned himself to death."

"Death," said one after another, standing and tearing the linen of their robes in a fierce gesture of aversion and a disclaiming and casting out of this man from the community of Israel. Death, death. The guards at the door repeated it. It echoed through the courtyard.

"Did he know this would follow when he said that?" one of the sons of Annas asked, rather shakenly. For if he did know, and still said it, was that not—no, not a proof but at least a possibility, that it might be true, that they, the priests, had failed to recognise their own?

"It was a challenge," said Caiaphas; "we had to accept it. Once a man has said that, either you must believe him or you must have him killed. And the consequences of believing him . . ."

"Yes, yes, impossible!" said the other, and then looked again at the prisoner and hesitated.

"It seems," said Caiaphas, "that we shall have to take that look off him," and then, louder: "we must formally condemn this blasphemy!" He took a couple of steps forward and hit the prisoner. It was not something he liked doing, but it was part of his duty as High Priest, and, yes, in a way an expression of his tremendous relief, his sense of a burden lifted. There might also, even among his friends and followers, be those who were shaken by what the prisoner had said; they would be thinking in terms, not of power, but of stories and prophecies: something not to do with religion in the sense that a priest of the Temple ought to know it. For the sake of those weaker brethren the prisoner must be spat upon, have his hair and clothes torn, have the look of assurance knocked off his face. That will become known, thought Caiaphas, and nobody will ever more dare to believe anything he has said or says.

Two

IN her sleep Claudia had heard the watchman calling
midnight. She had thrown her arms out, shoving
something away, something she couldn't see. Her arms
had pushed off the soft woollen shawl, dyed with stripes of
genuine murex purple and red, as befitted the wife of a
high-ranking Roman official, herself well born. One of the
slaves whose duty it was to watch all night had tiptoed over
and laid the shawl softly back in place; the girl was from
farther east, very gentle, very easily frightened, low voiced.
Barsiné was lucky to have been bought in by Lady Claudia
Procula's housekeeper. There is a certain measure of justice,
and even sometimes of mercy, in a respectable Roman
household.

During the next hour or so her mistress tossed and
sometimes muttered or whimpered in her sleep. Barsiné
wondered, anxiously, if she could have been bewitched. It
was so easy to say or do the unlucky thing and allow the
domination of the witch or the entry of evil spirits. Not that
this was how the Romans thought. Lord Pilate had a very
learned doctor on his staff who talked about fevers and
agues and gave powerful medicines, but no charms. Barsiné,
though, had sewn a charm on to the underside of the
beautiful, costly rug, a tiny charm but strong. When Lady
Claudia had distributed presents on her husband's name
day, Barsiné had spent half of hers on this charm. Not for
herself; but for Lady Claudia who had been so kind, who
had not whipped her even on the day she had been stupid
about the bath powder, Lady Claudia who had asked her if

she was tired, if she liked figs, if she could do Tyrian embroidery, just as if she'd been a real person, not a slave.

So when Lady Claudia woke right up, Barsiné was beside her in a moment, pulling out the lamp wick to make a bigger flame, then lighting another and moving over the charcoal brazier so that a pleasant warmth might be shed. Lady Claudia sat up against her pillows; she was older than Barsiné, but she still moved softly and quickly like a cat, a kind cat. Barsiné slipped another pillow behind her, then without a word brought over a little bowl of citron-scented warm water and a fine sponge. Lady Claudia smiled and reached out her wrists. She let Barsiné comb back her hair gently, gently, then she said: "Find me Hector, will you, Barsiné? Tell him I want him."

"With his tablets, my lady?"

"No. Perhaps yes. I don't know. If he's asleep tell him I'm so sorry, but I really need him."

"Of course, my lady!" Barsiné was shocked. After all, Hector was a slave, like herself. Why should Lady Claudia consider him in this way?

She ran out and barefoot down the half-lit passage. The Greek secretary, Hector, slept in a small cupboard of a room, among his writing things, on the master's side of the house; he might be wanted at any minute. He was a grave young man, not unhandsome, slave-born, the only child his parents had been allowed to keep; that was why they had named him, Homerically, Hector. He had been brought up to speak and write several languages, to be quick and docile. He had been shipped about the Empire from Rome to Marseilles to Alexandria to Syracuse to Athens to Jerusalem. It was all the same.

Barsiné opened the door, found the room dark and Hector asleep. She shook him. He turned over, smelt woman and made a grab at her. But she wasn't having any. "The mistress wants you," she said sharply, and he attempted nothing more except to touch her, as though by accident, in

the dark while he slipped on his tunic and put a comb
through his hair. One day perhaps the Procurator would let
him have a woman of his own, even if not, probably, such a
desirable one as Barsiné.

He came through to Lady Claudia's room and bowed. She
lay against the pillows, and the dark of her nipples showed
through the thin linen covering her uneasy breath. Sharply
he averted his thought. This was not a woman, but Lady
Claudia, the wife of the Procurator. Barsiné, though,
seemed to sense him; she took a scarf out of the chest and
arranged it neatly round her lady's shoulders and falling in
front where concealment should be.

"Tell me," said Lady Claudia, "why do the Jews dislike
us so much?"

"Perhaps," he said cautiously, "your ladyship may have
seen something—unpleasant?"

"It's not that," she said, "and nothing to do with—oh, our
visitors. But in little ways I always seem to be feeling it!
Nothing we do turns out right. My husband's water supply
scheme—you'd have thought they'd be grateful. Think of
the health it will bring; beautiful, fresh, mountain water in a
great aqueduct instead of these dirty wells."

"Yes, indeed, they are ungrateful," said Hector and shook
his head.

But she went on impatiently: "Come on; you know what's
happening, I'm sure you do! People are always hiding things
from me, and I have to know!"

"Do you order me to tell you, my lady?" said Hector. And
suddenly he thought he would really like her to know; she
might even help her husband to understand. Esdras, who
was secretary to Chuza the Treasurer, had suggested this to
him once; he had been scared to do anything about it. But
perhaps now was the chance.

"Yes, I do!" she said sharply.

He went on: "This is why, my lady. His Excellency the
Procurator has taken the Jewish Temple treasure to pay for

the aqueduct, and they are hurt and angry. It is money dedicated to their God. As though it were sacred to Apollo or to Venus Genetrix."

"Oh, I see," she said. "How odd. I never thought of that."

"And then, when he came, he brought the Standards of the Legions into the city of Jerusalem. They didn't like that either. They thought the Standards were another kind of God."

"Just because of the military ceremonies in connection with them? How very peculiar of them. It sounds as if this God of theirs must be a very jealous God."

"That is just what they say themselves," Hector said. "They are a very religious people. They have all kinds of customs, and the rest of us can't help breaking them, sometimes by accident, but sometimes—at least it seems so to them—on purpose."

"Yes," she said, thinking aloud to herself, "even our visitors seem to think that; so odd!" And then she went on suddenly: "Now tell me about these Essenes."

That was the last thing he had expected her to ask about. He didn't know what to say. How had she got to know about them? He glanced at Barsiné, but got nothing there. He felt cold and sleepy and aggrieved at having been pulled out of bed to talk about religions. If she'd had something else to think about—well, that wasn't her fault. He said cautiously: "It's one of these Jewish sects, but stricter than the others. They don't believe in marriage or—anything of the kind."

"Yes," said Claudia, "that's what I heard. They may have something there."

The secretary looked away. Nobody knew the habits of the Procurator better than he did. Normal, of course, highly normal. Nothing anybody could take exception to. Unless, possibly, a wife who happened to have—well, certain sensitivities. He went on: "They pray several times a day. They do not eat meat nor drink wine. They practise austerities of various kinds. And they hold all their property in common."

"Really?" she said. "That must be very amusing. Perhaps they haven't got much property to share."

"I don't expect so," he said.

"There are several of these sects, aren't there?" she asked, settling down among her pillows.

He moved a little nearer the brazier; might as well try to keep warm, anyway. "I understand that is so," he said. "For instance there is a sect called the New Alliance. They are equally strict. There is a gathering of members every day for discussion and perhaps prayer. I've heard that anyone who goes to sleep in the meeting gets punished."

"They are very superstitious, aren't they?" she said uneasily. "I mean, they believe in visions and what they call Messengers?"

"Yes, but equally they hold certain philosophical ideas which are also held by the Epicureans." He did not, however, say that one of these was the doctrine of the brotherhood of man: precluding the possibility of slavery. To a Roman, that idea would seem as crazy as visions.

She fidgeted with the edge of her shawl, then asked: "This new Galilean prophet—Jesus of Nazareth—does he belong to any of them?"

"I doubt it," he said, a little uncomfortably—why should she have heard of him? "He goes about the country with his followers, mostly country people, eating and drinking and talking to anyone. The Pharisees—you remember, Lady Claudia, those are the very religious Jews who take so much trouble about their rituals and are unwilling to be seen with any of the occupying power—they don't approve of this Jesus; he is not as strict as they are over a number of things."

"Did you hear about his bringing a dead man back to life?"

"That kind of thing has been said about a number of these Eastern magicians and prophets, Lady Claudia. One would hardly credit it oneself."

The girl Barsiné spoke: "I met someone who had come from the same village—Bethany—she says it's quite true!"

"Well, there seem to be two opinions," said Lady Claudia, "but I would like to have it arranged for me to meet this prophet. Or is he as silly about women as some of these extremists are?"

"No," said the secretary. "In fact I know of one or two very sensible women who are in touch with his organisation. Would you—were you thinking of suggesting, Lady Claudia, that I might sound one of them?"

"Yes, Hector, that's just what I want you to do. Have you anyone in mind?"

He hesitated: "Well, yes, as a matter of fact I have. There is Madame Joanna, the wife of Chuza, Herod's Treasurer."

"I'd never have guessed it!" said Lady Claudia. "She always looks so stiff and solemn at receptions. You know, this prophet was talking at a street corner one day when I was going by in my litter. I made them stop for a few minutes. Of course I couldn't make out what he was saying, but he looked—oh well, he looked like someone who has had some kind of strange experience. Not a handsome face, and he didn't look at all strong, but of course it's an unhealthy life going round preaching and arguing and having stones thrown. There was something about him—I recalled his look just now when I was dreaming." She frowned and pushed her hair back from her brow.

"Oh, if only he hasn't bewitched you, my lady!" cried Barsiné, suddenly worried. Let him raise the dead if he likes, but don't let him interfere with his betters!

"Silly child!" said Lady Claudia, and reached out a hand to Barsiné, who laid a soft warm kiss into the palm. "Now, bring me a nice cup of milk with just that much spiced wine in it. And you go back to bed, Hector. But see if you can put me in touch with Chuza's wife quite soon. It would be interesting. One feels so cut off here. Perhaps if you told her I wanted to know about this prophet, she might be less standoffish than the rest of the Jews? What do you think?"

"I'm sure you are right, Lady Claudia," said Hector with some enthusiasm, and the prospect of getting back to bed. He would see Esdras early in the morning and get it arranged. The lady Joanna had plenty of sense; she might be able to explain to Lady Claudia just which of her husband's schemes were particularly tactless. That is, if the Old Man happened to be willing to pay any attention to her. She'd a bad habit of catching him just at the wrong moment. But there, how was she to know if one of the popsies had played him up? If Lady Claudia could manage to get on to his level a bit more. Not that it was his affair to make things too easy for his owners. Still, she might be worse, a lot worse. And Esdras would be pleased if something came of this. You never knew.

Three

IT was a very small room for all the things and people it had in it. There were chests and cooking pots and jars for storing food and sheepskin coats hanging up; there were hooks into the ceiling beams, and strung from them were baskets of dried beans and figs, bunches of herbs and strings of onions. The tiny window in the back wall was shuttered against the cold. The side wall, which was built into the rock of the hill, had a recess in it with rugs and cushions, some covered with coarse needlework, heaped up, along with a coil of rope and some baskets. On the floor below it, lying on a rug, two women were asleep, or rather two hunched bundles, from which only a few grey wisps of hair showed on one of them, an old, pale foot on the other. A third, much younger woman was awake and sitting on the floor slowly grinding up some kind of grain into meal, something she could feel her way to do in the half dark. For the one small lamp stood in a niche of the mud brick wall on the men's side of the room.

In the middle of the mud floor, a small fire in the sunk hearth smouldered away, giving little heat. The two men sat on stools beside it, occasionally sticking out a hand to warm. One of them raised his head, thinking he heard the steps coming to the door. But they passed on, and his neck dropped back into weariness. Then at last, when they had almost dozed off again, the steps did come and the rattle at the latch. One of them got up and opened the door. "You, James," he said.

The woman who was grinding stopped, holding the pestle

still in the mortar. The man who had come in was thin, with long, straggly hair; he looked old for his years, older, the woman thought once more, so much older than his brother, although he was more than a year younger. He wore no wool nor beasts' skins, but linen, worn in places into holes that had not been darned but roughly pulled together. He said to the men: "It has happened after all; they did arrest him."

The young woman, who was a virgin, stayed very still; she had thought it would happen, and yet—there had always been some other possibility. The man went on: "He said— he said before the judges that he was the Messiah, the One that was foretold. Have we wronged him then, Simon? Was he—after all—the most Pure One?"

Simon, the younger brother, the one who had carried on the family business, broke a thick twig in his hands and dropped it into the fire. "We shall have to tell our mother; and we talked her down."

Both of them looked at the sleeping women. At last the younger brother said: "Not yet. Not till we know more. She —she will try to make us do something."

"Doing! Doing!" said the older man. "Women can never stop this doing!" He glared across at the young woman, who dropped her eyes, aware of how he thought of her and yet rebelling at it, but not enough to speak. There was another to whom women were not the impure, the enemy; for him, every woman was a sister, whose hand he could take.

The third man, who had been silent in front of his country cousins, even though it was his house, spoke in a harsh whisper, looking into the ashes: "I thought he was the King. And now you say he is a prisoner."

"He too has gone that road," said James whom some called Judge, and the echoes of what he said came back into the other minds. For his brother was not the first of the Teachers of Righteousness to fall into the hands of the Children of Darkness.

"I thought he would set us free from all our oppressors. And establish his Kingdom that will—that would—" the man stumbled for words, "—that could be the end of Romans and these other ones of our own blood . . . that I hate!"

"That are hated by the All Just. Spat out of his mouth! Like unclean flesh."

"He said he was the King," the man went on. The older brother, James, looked away, his face twisted as though by some pain in the body.

It was Simon, the younger one, who answered: "It was others that said so. Not he. He said he was the Son of Man, the one that was foretold."

"What did he mean, Simon bar Joseph? Why did he never speak plain, telling us when he would raise his army? He was your brother, Simon bar Joseph, you must have known! Was he the one he let us think he was?"

"We never knew," Simon said. "When someone is your brother you cannot see him plain. How could we be the ones to know?"

"I knew," said the woman, softly. The old ones were still asleep.

"You," said James, quite quietly, and it was worse than if he had abused her.

Another man came in, an older one; he too wearing the chilly, much scrubbed linen of the Essenes or near Essenes. He did not even notice the women. "James, son of Joseph," he said, "your brother—but you know. This is a very terrible world. He tried to work in and through it. That was wrong. Now it has him between its teeth."

The look of deep pain was still on James. "He should have known!" he said. "But it was as if—he could not hate the world. As it must be hated. The world and the flesh: which torture us, in order that we may turn from them towards what alone has value." He seemed to choke on the words. "What will they do to Jesus, our brother?"

"The worst," said the older man, almost with satisfaction.

"Yet through that, he will surely lose his trust in the world and by the end he will see the way of light."

"He did somehow trust the world," said Simon, shaking his head. "He could never have done business that way. You know, he never got any kind of reference nor guarantee, but just put his trust in the ones that chose to follow him. And where are they all now? Run like rats. But it wasn't only people. He'd go up to a stray dog, only fit to throw stones at, and touch it and trust it, an unclean dog! Flowers, common wild flowers off the hills, he'd touch them the same way. Or children. Anything that was just part of the world. He loved it all like—like our father used to love a good table or a set of stools he'd made himself. Touching along the grain of the wood, that way he had."

Once more the young woman, who was called Mary, wondered about that father of his who had died when he was still a lad, and whom he remembered—yes, as did all of them—as wise and gentle. He had meant, maybe, more to the boys than to his widow, who had been so busy bringing them all up. A good man cherishes his children and must in turn be cherished by his wife, if she is a good wife. And, as she was thinking this, suddenly one of the sleeping bundles stirred, sat up, pushed hands over face, tucked hair in under veil, and then looked quick and piercingly from James to Simon and back. Both men shifted a little as though a light had blazed in the dark little room. "He has been taken," the woman said.

With a grave movement of his head her next elder son admitted that this was so.

"So, what are you doing?" she asked.

"What can we do?" said Simon. "If he is what he says, he need only speak the Names of the angels . . ." He shivered; it was all getting beyond him.

"But if he does not choose to do that?" said the young Mary, almost to herself. She had no doubts. This would be easy for the one who had dealt with her own . . . weakness.

Which some had called devils. She began to think about that
while the others spoke across her, James telling his mother
all he knew about the arrest last night in the market garden
across on the other side of the Kedron valley.

It was something which had shadowed all her childhood,
growing worse as she herself grew into a tall maiden. Her
father, back in Magdala, had sacrificed and spent silver and
gold, both at home and in Jerusalem, uselessly. He had even
gone to magicians, although it went against his principles;
great Names had been invoked over her, signs and charms
drawn or painted on and around her. But she had screamed
and screamed, in red and purple and black, in hard squares
and cutting triangles, and she had gone on seeing those
images which had forced her into the screaming. Until he
came, and everything went quiet and grey-blue like early
morning and had stayed so. So now, if he had told her that
he would rather die quietly than raise legions of terrible
screaming angels, she would have understood. But would his
brothers understand?

.   .   .   .   .

Another man had come in. She did not know who he was,
but certainly he was not one of the Pure Ones; he had given
her a hot look, the kind that seemed to go straight through
her clothes, down into her flesh that softened horribly like
meat under a hammer. She pulled her veil forward and
went on grinding at the grain with hands that shook. In the
old days Mary of Magdala had not been used to the houses
and doings of the poor, the open lusts of the Amharetz, the
common people. Her parents had been among the well-to-do
of that flourishing little town; there were vineyards, an olive
grove and cornland behind them; she had not been aware of
the other life which had gone on outside the walls of her
parents' house. When her father had brought her to this new
healer, it had never entered his head that she might leave
them for him and his folk. There had been a marriage in

3—BYK

course of arrangement; once the devils had been driven out she was indeed desirable. The marriage brokers had brought presents; she should stand under the canopy, where these hot looks were not shaming but lawful—or so it was said.

Yet that was not the way things had worked out. She had left her home to follow this one from whom she did not get hot looks, but a kindness that did not seem to be different for man or woman. At first her parents had forbidden her to go. But they too were shaken in their minds by what he did and said and how he appeared to live. If he were indeed the one that was foretold, who would end the miseries of Israel, and their daughter were to find favour in his sight. . . . Her mother still wept and wailed, but Mary had left the house in Magdala and here she was now in a back street of the Ophel, the workers' quarter of Jerusalem, seeing and hearing things which she had never even thought of.

Not that this house was too bad. It lay up the hill a little in a kind of back yard of its own. There was a passage with arches, and in one place a green creeper bursting over a high wall. When she had gone out to buy bread and draw water at the well—she had never done it before, but at least it was a burden she could take off the older women—she had found it difficult at first to find her way back, and she was scared to ask. In the old days people had never looked at her this way, nor used their voices to hurt her. That seemed to go with the street mud caking on her ankles and the smell of filth at the corners. Once an elderly man whom she had thought safe to ask had laughed at her, then pinched her and tried to pull her into a doorway. A thick veil helped, for behind that she could pretend to be old and not desirable. But the danger from men was always about, like the smell in the street drains, and as foul, although it seemed there were women who dealt in this abomination and, in turn, made other women appear hateful to men. In the old days she had heard them whispered about and shuddered at, but now she had seen them, heard and smelt them, felt their touch brush across her—yet they must be her sisters according to the knowledge she now had. And so were the men her brothers. Yet how—how to prove it? For such things must be in action.

She remembered now his anger with her when she had spoken with shuddering disgust of such a one, of the defiling touch. For him defilement came, not from the unclean touch but from the unclean thing in the heart of the touched leaping out to welcome it. Put that right and there could be neither defilement nor need of cleansing. But how to know if one was clean-hearted?

. . . . .

The room was packed now. People had come in out of the night and the crowded city, most of them with Galilean accents. Simon was speaking earnestly with his mother. The other woman was moaning to herself, quietly. The men were arguing. There was one who went nagging on about the King; a king who had to be crowned and die on a three-branched tree; something to do with the springing of the corn. He quoted what seemed to be texts, and yet somehow, and in spite of King David the dancer, it was not a Jewish idea, but something from outside and underneath. Her Jesus had never called himself king, and had laughed when others used the word to him; that was enough for Mary.

Then there was a louder clatter at the door, another Galilean voice, that of her friend Rocky the fisherman, the one who didn't look at her the hot way, nor yet the icy way of the pure. But now he looked as though something terrible had happened to him. He began to talk about the trial, brokenly; he said what words had been spoken, as though he were bound to remember those words for ever. And suddenly he caught hold of James: "Look, you've got the name of being just. Judge, I've heard you called. I want you to say what you think of me: straight. Look: I gave him my word I'd stand by him—always. I meant it—see? Said I'd die for him."

"You believed everything he said about himself?" said James.

"And everything we said about him—yes!" said Rocky.

"And so?"

"I was scared. Me, Rocky. Scared to my guts. You don't know—it was all that picturing of the Kingdom. Glory and marching in and—him being recognised in our own Jerusalem for what he was. I used to think that a day would come when everyone would see: sudden. And bow down. The High Priest kneeling in front of him. Everything forgiven and starting again clean and new like a Spring morning. Pictures. And then we saw him taken and tied. So when they asked me if I was one of his crowd, I said no. Three separate times I did that—trying to get away."

"Away from my brother whom you called Master and Teacher," said James, painfully.

"We called him more than that!" Rocky said, and his hands closed, tugging at his rough hair.

"Even if my brother were none of these things," James the Judge went on, his mouth in a hard line, "he might have expected better from his followers, from men of Israel. In the time of the Maccabees men were not afraid of death."

"That wasn't the kind of fear," said Rocky; "it was—fear of his not being the one we thought. . . ." Suddenly he plunged away from James towards the women. "Mother," he said to the older one, "you heard . . ." She put her hands on to his head, where he had knelt to catch her round the knees; her fingers trembled a little in his hair. "But I'll do something," he said; "I will. Tell me, could this have been sent to try me, to see if I am a man?"

"It could," she said.

"Very well," he said. "Now listen. This lot aren't going to condemn him. They'd like to, they'd like to eat him alive, but they're going to get the Romans to do it. So they'll take him there, or maybe first to Herod. There'll be the Temple guards, but if we attacked, all of us, we'd get him away." He turned round. "Who's got a sword?" Several of the men answered eagerly. "That's what he meant—to shame me—so I could see how low I could fall—and then me to be the one to get him away, to save him, to start the kingdom! That's what he wants—I see it all so plain now!"

"But Rocky!" said the young Mary, low and urgently. "Rocky, are you sure it's what he wants? If he'd meant to escape, wouldn't he have saved himself, wouldn't he have called up the Powers?" She found the men were listening to her, first Rocky, then the others. "Oh Rocky," she said, "perhaps it's not what he wants!"

Rocky answered very simply: "But it's what I want, Miss Mary. We can't be certain about him. But—but—surely you don't want him to die?"

It was terrible, but his saying that made her choke and then the tears came. How much she didn't want him to die! But if that was what he wanted himself—for some reason that she half saw. . . . Yet Rocky might be right, good, straight Rocky, the one she'd always trusted because he loved their Jesus in the same way that she did herself. She felt the older woman holding on to her arm, trying to tell her something—but what? She didn't know; she had always been a little afraid of his mother, this woman who had been so violent a patriot, so beautiful in her country way—or so the older people said—who had been so certain that it would be her own, eldest son who would save Israel. And yet it had been his father whom he had always cared for. "No," said the older woman, "no!" But what was she saying "no" to?

The men were talking, gathered round Rocky. One of them ran out and came back with a bundle of spears, old things, one of the shafts cracked and useless. "I'll do it!" said Rocky, panting. Yes, they were going to do something, action—no more words.

Only James stood apart, his pain unassuaged. At last he said what was in his mind: "Simon bar Jonas, the Law says

'Thou shalt not kill'. My brother taught that the Law was to be kept above all. Whatever else he taught, whatever new, doubtful things, at least he always taught that."

"He broke the Law when it needed to be broken," said Rocky sturdily. "He said that a man could break the Law if he knew well what he was doing, if he knew it was for something—something beyond all rules. That time they said we were Sabbath breaking . . ."

"This is different," said the Judge, "as you know well, and who are you to say if a great Commandment is to be broken, you, Simon, coward—out of your own mouth!"

"Because of that I must do this," said Rocky, "and I am going to be in front."

That should hearten his mother, thought the young Mary, glancing sideways towards her, but finding that the man who had come in earlier and looked at her had edged himself between them in the half dark. She found herself looking into his hot eyes, and the terrible melting feeling began in her bones, as though she wanted him to touch her. She snatched herself away from it, catching her veil between her teeth. But the man was whispering. "I can pull this off," he said; "they can't." She didn't answer. He went on: "Do you want me to?"

Should she even speak? At last she whispered, not looking: "Who are you?"

"Malachi bar Joses," he said, "I'm—a patriot, see? I was never a follower of this one they've taken, but if we get him away from them—well, that'll be different. He'd be our leader—I've heard him preach, saw him in the Temple lashing out good and strong—our leader against the occupying forces. See? Against the ones that have got him now, the ones that go arse-licking to this Pilate! Sadducees!" The word came hissing out.

"You would—follow him?" she whispered.

"I would," he said. "I followed the other Jesus—Jesus bar Rabban."

"Who was taken at the riots?"

"Yes, at the tower! I was there, I fought. Just you look, girl." He bared his arm and there was a horrible raised scar, red and angry-looking still. "They got Bar Rabban. He was wounded; one of those filthy Romans speared him through the leg, and he's a prisoner still. But I got away. And I know all the boys who'd fight again if they saw half a chance. Most of the Quarter would fight—if I said so!"

"And then—follow him?"

"I tell you, he'd be our leader! Isn't that straight? My boys would do it against all the Temple guards! That lot of country clots—they couldn't. Only get themselves killed. And maybe him too. So—shall I do it?"

She began to tremble. She began to know why he was asking her. It was so dark and crowded in the room; nobody saw how close he was edging in. Now his arm was sliding round her, the whispering hot in her ear: "You're Mary from Magdala, aren't you? A real lady! I want you, I want a real lady, a dainty darling, never had one yet. You'd be tender as a sucking lamb. You'd try and fight me, wouldn't you, but when I'd got you down, oh you'd be soft. . . ." She had her hands stuffed over her ears, she cowered back against the wall. If only one of the older women would come—or Rocky! Suddenly he caught her wrists and pulled them away. "There! I've frightened you. Never mind, I'll go gentle when the time comes. But you're to say—see? Am I to rescue him? Shall I stop them killing your Jesus?"

"Oh!" she said, "oh—do it for *him*!"

"I'd risk getting killed myself—some of us are bound to get killed. Am I to get nothing out of it? Nothing?" His voice had the common, Jerusalem street accent, but it was going soft at her. "It's because you're a lady," he said, "and me only a poor man. A poor patriot. Nothing but my sword and my strength—for Israel. And for your Jesus if you say the word."

"You are my brother," she said faintly. What ought she

to do? How far it was from her father's house where everything was just so, where she would be told with certainty what was right! She had let all that go to follow the Messiah. It was bad that this man should think of her as a fine lady; it made her feel in the wrong. He was one of the poor, whom she must not despise. And it was in her hands whether or not the one foretold, the Messiah, was to die—probably tortured, she had heard what they were saying about that—the one who had healed her, had it in him to heal thousands more! Was this a test for her as the other thing had been a test for Rocky? She didn't know! Only that she must give anything for *him*.

"Well?" the man whispered.

"Do it," she answered. She felt his hands press quickly round her, hard and hot with possession, over her shoulders, arms, breasts, and then he was away, talking to the other men, and out through the door into the night street and running. Oh, what had she promised?

Four

IT was almost time for the midnight guard to be changed, and the dawn guard to come over from the Antonia and take it on. Naturally the official Roman residence at Jerusalem, which used to be the Palace of the old Herod, was well guarded, not by natives, but by legionaries: men who were not likely to do too much fraternising. Their headquarters were at Cæsarea on the coast, but that wasn't where trouble was likeliest, so there was always at least one cohort in Jerusalem, and now, over these tricky days of Passover, at least three. A couple of thousand legionaries, fully equipped and holding all the vital spots, were enough to keep down ten times their own number of disorganised, quarter-armed rioters—if there did happen to be rioting. And the sight of them marching up from the coast, a hard, menacing glitter along the dusty roads, was salutary in itself.

The Procurator was quite popular with the soldiers; they thought it a bit of a joke, the way he had treated these Jews, not standing any nonsense. And the pay came through regularly. They were, of course, part of the Syrian command, and might be recalled for frontier duty at any time. At least that was the theory. But a good many of the Raging Tenth had been in Judæa during most of their service.

Cnæus Musius, the centurion, was talking to one of his senior men, warming his hands at the brazier in the little guard hut. Outside they could hear the regular stamp and clatter of the guard marching and counter-marching. Cnæus was talking about his experience up in the Syrian mountains, some way to the north of Jerusalem: "This Baal

33

of theirs, he's certainly something. You know, Quintus, we
haven't got all the answers."

"Haven't got any of them, I'd say," said the other man.

"This Baal, now—he's another shape for our own Jupiter.
Or the old Zeus. It seems as though you get the same
Immanence, in mountains. Doliche, Olympos, those great
Cretan jags. And now in Syria; that tremendous bloody
range with snow on it and the green country under it
powdered pink with apricot trees. Yes, in the mountains. A
presence, if I can put it that way, demanding worship."

"I believe in luck," said the other soldier, "but you can do
things about it. Force it your way."

"There's too much in the world that we don't know
about," said the centurion. "The sea and its winds, the
metals twisting under the earth. Luck! One's killed and
another's spared, often a worse one. One woman slips her
kids with no bother. Another—and it may be the Emperor's
wife at that—gets the thing stuck and then she lies and
screams for days. And dies in the end." He scowled, as
though at some memory.

"That's nature," said the older man; "I've seen the same
thing with a mare. A good mare. It's what people do to one
another that has me scared. Tyrants out East getting their
fun out of torturing their own brothers and sisters. And
even in Rome. I had a letter from my young brother, all
about this Divine Emperor of ours. . . ."

"You'd better watch out what that brother of yours
writes! Safe with me." The other man laughed. "You can
laugh, but you don't know who mayn't be an informer; yes,
even here! So I'm warning you. Oh well, what I was saying
was that with the world being so chancy and on the whole
things apt to turn out bad, one wants something to hold on
to—a power beyond those powers we know. I've never been
one for the Mysteries, not for the old ones anyway, Eleusis,
and that: awkward for a soldier, you've got to take a lot of
oaths which might stop you doing your duty at certain times.

No, I wouldn't advise anyone in the army to think along those lines. But that Baal up in the Syrian mountains, I can tell you I wasn't ashamed to offer him a sacrifice."

"What did he want—sheep?"

"That kind of thing. Seems he can do big things for the crops and beasts. And they depend on their exports."

The other man was chewing over something: "You know that goddess of theirs at Carthage. Kind of bird, she is: Tanit. Doesn't do to make her angry or she sends dreams— the worst kind. Well, I had a year's service there; thought I'd better not take any chances, went along to do a sacrifice. But do you know what kind of sacrifice Tanit wants? Babies. Little, scrunchy babies. Squash them and burn them. You could buy a baby cheap to sacrifice; there was a whole cage of slaves kept for breeding them. They'd ask you to go in the cage, too! But it wasn't what I liked. The babies would have died anyway, but—well, I didn't sacrifice to old Tanit."

"Quite right," said the centurion. "One can't go all the way with natives. These Jews, now—they always object to everything. They won't let a stranger any farther than the outside court of their Temple, no, not even if he comes with the best of intentions. I'd be quite prepared to say that their God was another aspect of Jupiter. But it wouldn't please them. No, they wouldn't say thank you for that."

"Silly sods," said the older man. Then he felt under the metal flaps of his kilt and rolled up the leg of the leather shorts he wore underneath it, regular service dress. "See that," he said. There was a curious scar fairly high up on his thigh, reddish and shaped like a pair of stag's horns. "That was one of these goddesses. I got it in Gaul."

"You've been about, haven't you!"

"Yes, yes, and a nice little native wife wherever I went. Good as gold, most of them. But this was early on, near Lugudunum. Wooded country, and that great river, can't remember what they called it. This goddess of theirs was the forest lady, looked after the wild beasts. Or killed them.

According as. Or took the shape of one of them or turned
people into them. I got interested. You know what it is.
When one's a boy one doesn't realise the beastliness of the
world, and I'd had a good home. When I went into the army
—well, it wasn't quite what I'd pictured. Not that I'd mind
now."

"Things come one's way in the course of duty," said the
centurion. "Yes?"

"Well, I got tangled up a bit with this native goddess
because it seemed as if she could make sense of some of the
beastliness. And this was her sign. They like a bit of blood
and pain, do the Great Mothers."

"You got off light," said the centurion. "If it had been
Cybele, now!"

"Ah. She'd have gone six inches higher. But this—it
seemed wonderful at the time. Seemed to change my luck. I
felt, if you take me, that I'd done something to bind her to
me, through my own flesh. Then the legion was shifted,
pretty suddenly. I'd a nice girl, too—long hair, kind of
tawny yellow like these Gaulish girls have. I never knew
what happened to her."

Another, younger soldier came in, saluted the centurion
and then blew on his fingers, trying to warm them. He was
coming on duty from the Antonia fortress at the corner of
the Temple hill, where most of the Roman garrison were
quartered. The centurion asked him if they'd seen or heard
anything out of the way from the look-out there. "Not a
cheep, sir," said the man, "except that there were some
lights in one of the big houses."

"Which one?"

"It belongs to one of those priests. Annas, is it, sir? I
thought they might be keeping this feast or whatever it is."

"They're Sadducees. Our so-called friends! I heard they
didn't keep it till this evening. There have been some
squabbles about it among the Jews, so I hear. If it wasn't
that it would be something else. Nothing more?"

"No, sir. And I was to remind you about the fodder issue for the last lot of horses."

"That's right. As soon as the gates are opened and the country carts start coming in, we'll do a requisition. They may have some green-stuff from the valley. We'd better get enough for a week."

The older soldier looked up and said to the younger one: "We were talking about luck. What do you do for your luck, young Marcus?"

The young man stiffened and said: "I do what a soldier should do!"

"Oh, you're one of *them*," said the older man, "my mistake." And he made a noise like a crow.

"Shut up!" said the younger one, "if we didn't have some decent beliefs—! At least part of the army is clean!"

The centurion came between them. He realised how passionate the followers of the Saviour Mithras were apt to become, if they felt that they or their god was being insulted. They were usually good soldiers, though. He told the younger man to take a squad round the Procurator's residence, going through all the courtyards and keeping his eyes skinned, but not making too much noise. "We can't have Lady Claudia disturbed," he said, "but at the same time we can't have thieves—or murderers. And you never know."

The younger man saluted again and marched off. The midnight guard dismissed and the dawn guard took over. A friend of the centurion turned up, and they made bets on the cock-fights there were going to be that evening; drove the Jews half crazy to have them on the Sabbath. Which was a joke in itself.

. . . . .

The squad went through the outer courtyard without seeing anyone, but found someone walking across the inner one. But, challenged, it turned out to be only Hector, the secretary. "What are you doing at this time of night?" said young Marcus.

"As a matter of fact," said Hector, "I'm on my way to see a colleague at Chuza's. You know what it is; His Excellency starts work at cockcrow, or at least he's liable to, and I want to get this message across before I'm stuck."

"What is it—official?"

"Kind of," said Hector and winked. If that gave a wrong impression it was just too bad.

"I wouldn't have thought Chuza——"

"No, you wouldn't, would you? But there it is."

"Of course, with him being treasurer to the Fox, he might have things up his sleeve. Well, tell the centurion I challenged you. I might as well get the credit."

Hector duly reported at the guardhouse. Somebody had just come in with a message and he waited for a moment till the centurion had thought it over. "All right if I go on?" he asked.

"To Chuza's, eh?" said the centurion. Then he remarked: "He might be interested in this trial that's been going on. An awkward time to have it with all these pilgrims and everyone getting worked up. But these Sadducees might just have done it on purpose to get us into trouble. We haven't heard the last of it, that's one thing certain."

"What trial would that be?" the secretary asked, respectfully.

"Old man Annas and that son-in-law of his, Caiaphas, have got hold of some kind of religious agitator who calls himself a king and a son of God and goodness knows what else. Talks about tearing down the Temple and building it up again in three days. Always quoting these old prophecies."

"Sounds like that prophet John—the one Herod had executed two or three years ago. They seem to breed them here."

"True enough. Small nations get prophets. Look how they

used to happen even in Rome when we were still a small state. Now we don't need them any longer."

"No. You have administrators now." Suddenly the centurion wondered if His Excellency's secretary was cheeking him. But the man went on very seriously: "And the Jews have been—unfortunate."

"They've come in the way of big empires. Bad luck being where they are, between us and Parthia, so to speak. So they run to these prophets who say it'll be all right one day."

"Who say there's something more powerful than big empires."

"Well—that's not sensible."

"Is it this new prophet Jesus of Nazareth they've got hold of? It is! Well, he said something of the kind."

"No wonder he's in trouble, then. Looks like a case for His Excellency. You'd better be trotting along, Hector, or you'll find the news has spread and the Jerusalem mob's getting busy. And a nasty lot they are!"

"Thank you," said Hector, "but you will naturally have no trouble in dealing with them?"

"Naturally not!" said the centurion shortly, and motioned Hector away. You couldn't exactly treat him as a slave, because, after all, he was one of the Procurator's most valuable possessions. But sometimes Cnæus Musius wanted to kick him in the teeth.

Hector, obscurely feeling this, hurried. Besides, if the Jerusalem mob was going to move, there would be danger; the mob wouldn't distinguish one foreigner from another. The people were sore still about that Tower of Siloam business. It was so easy to get killed. And apparently so irrevocable. If you were the Divine Emperor they put up statues, made you into a constellation perhaps. Chilly to be a constellation. Fixed and staring at all the things you used to touch and hold. How nice if the Divine Emperors had really all been turned into stars, having to keep their places up there, nailed on to the heavens. And His Excellency the Procurator of Judæa, Pontius Pilate, along with them.

He made his way quickly across Jerusalem, through the dark, twisty, up-and-down streets. Luckily it was a fine night, though still so cold, and the low moon lighted the upper part of the walls and made a silver haze above them. The house was dark, but he knew the small side door and the old woman who kept it. He knocked in the way that meant he was a friend. She opened, and after a little talk went off to fetch his friend Esdras, who came running, at the same time fastening the belt round his long woollen coat that was embroidered handsomely at the corners, as befitted the secretary of such an important person as Chuza, Steward and Treasurer to the Tetrarch, Herod Antipas.

The two secretaries talked for a few minutes, and Esdras was enthusiastic over the idea of Madame Joanna meeting Lady Claudia. Yes, it might be most helpful. He would have a consultation with her as soon as possible. Then Hector mentioned that the Sadducees had got hold of this new prophet, Jesus of Nazareth, and had been trying him.

Esdras stiffened and bit his lip: "On what charge?"

"I don't know," Hector said. "Sedition, I suppose."

"Sedition—against you?"

"Against Rome," Hector said. "You might remember, Esdras, that I'm only a slave."

Esdras patted him on the shoulder: "I know you aren't a Roman, anyway, Hector. But this news will—yes, interest Madame Joanna. I think she would want me to go up and tell her at once. I wonder if it was a legal court; it mightn't have been. You'd better get back quickly, Hector. There may be considerable feeling over this and I wouldn't like you to be killed, whoever else is."

Five

"IT will be light in less than an hour," said Caiaphas, "and we must make our decision." He looked round at the others. "In my own mind the thing is quite straightforward. This is a Roman province: unfortunately no doubt. Nor does anyone deplore it more bitterly than I do. But there are certain consequences of that which we can and shall use. This man has claimed to be the anointed, the ruler of Israel, the son of God." He looked all round. There was his father-in-law, Annas, two uncles, a brother-in-law, and various cousins and cousins-in-law. They should be solid.

But suddenly a cousin threw up his head and spoke, white-faced: "But if he *is* the son of God . . ."

Caiaphas looked at him for a long minute, smiling a little; gradually the other one's head drooped. Caiaphas said comfortably: "There have been priests and teachers and magicians before; they have made this claim more or less. They have come, sooner or later, into conflict with the authorities. They have been disposed of. The world has gone on."

Annas said: "We shall have difficulties. The mob is on his side."

"I think they can be deflected," Caiaphas said. "Remember, he never promised to lead them to victory."

"He never even tried to stir them up," said another man.

"Oh, I agree, Eleazar," said Caiaphas. "On certain charges he is quite innocent. You will remember that we were not able to prove sorcery, my original idea. The witnesses let me down badly. Yes. A pity, for it would have put people thoroughly against him if it could have been proved. But he was so obviously nothing of the kind. Oh yes, he is innocent of all that. It cannot be helped."

"But if he is innocent, how can we condemn him?"

"He started raising the dead, you know. Once people begin to do that they undermine all civil authority, which rests ultimately on the death sanction."

"Are we sure he did that?"

"My informants at Bethany were reasonably definite. Besides—he is beginning to have a very large following, whether he wants it or not. This would be bound to come to the knowledge of the occupying authorities within a few months at most, and we would be held responsible. It would be an excuse for the Procurator to make further restrictions. As you know, he already keeps some of our most precious vestments in the fortress—merely lends them on certain occasions, to us, their owners! He might do worse. I can imagine him claiming—to overstep the boundaries, to seize on yet more of our holy objects and places. We have a duty to stop that happening, even if it means the death of one relatively innocent person."

"That is so," Annas said. "We who are in a special relation with the Lord our God and with our people, we must take the burden of our responsibilities."

"That brings me to the main point," Caiaphas said. He wanted to make this very clear, not to let it be deflected. And they were all tired. He clapped his hands for a servant and told him to have some wine heated and take it round. This was an inner room, beyond the hall of judgment, pleasantly frescoed in a pattern of formal vine branches. The prisoner was in yet another room off the hall of judgment, but alone, cold and tied to the ring in the wall.

Caiaphas said: "Now listen: let us forget about Messiah and such. The real charge does not directly concern us. It does concern the Romans. It is blasphemy against this Emperor of theirs, whom, as you know, they claim to be a god." He said this with a curious dry disgust that was echoed in the faces of his hearers. But the tools that come to the hand must be used, although dirty. He went on: "You all heard this Jesus claiming that he is the anointed one, that is to say the King. It may be that he does not even think of his kingdom as Judæa, but that is how it must seem to the Romans. It is blasphemy against their idol, the Emperor, and is punishable by death. The Procurator is bound to take this view if we bring the prisoner before him."

"But if he denies our accusation?" someone remarked uneasily.

"He will not deny it," said Caiaphas, "or if he does it will be in riddles that the Roman is too stupid to understand." He looked round again and as he looked two men came in together. They also were wearing priestly clothes, which had got them through the guard.

One of them spoke: "Caiaphas, we hear you have been holding a trial."

"That is so, Joseph bar Achim," said Caiaphas.

"Yourselves alone!" said the man whom Caiaphas had addressed. He was a big man with a black, curly beard. "Do you claim that it was legal?"

"It was not an important trial," said Caiaphas. "Would you call it important to try a crazy Galilean carpenter? Important enough for the Pharisees to notice it?" He bowed ironically.

Joseph said: "I would have been there, but the news did not get to me at Arimathæa, where I was keeping Passover, until past midnight. And I would never have agreed."

The other man, who was thin and grey-haired, said: "You may be doing something terribly wrong, Caiaphas, in order to play politics with the Romans." Caiaphas laughed, and so did some of his relations. The man, whose name was Nicodemus, went on: "I saw Jesus of Nazareth several times, questioned him, spoke to him openly. He—he may be what is said."

"It seems strange that you Pharisees should think that,

when I remember how he abused you," Caiaphas said with a certain satisfaction, and he repeated some of the things which this same Jesus had been saying about the Pharisees. Wicked and adulterous . . . who slam the door of the kingdom of heaven against everyone else . . . fools and blind . . . full of extortion and luxury and every kind of uncleanness. . . .

Nicodemus interrupted him: "I know. He said things like that to me that night I first went to him, in a small village near Capernaum. I was very much upset. We had been somewhat shocked by a good many of his actions. Over prayer; over defilement; over the unclean sick and women; above all perhaps over the Romans and those who act as their agents. We thought he had gone much too far in even speaking to them. Added to that, we thought he had been saying things deliberately in order to try to put us in the wrong. We thought he was too much occupied with illiterates and such. I tried to argue along these lines. Yes, I began to argue with him. But he had had certain experiences which made my arguments completely pointless. He told me I was not fit to understand what he was talking about. Whereas some quite ordinary, common people who were going about with him were spiritually prepared to understand. That hurt at the time; it was more than I could take. But I thought over what he had said, cruel though it seemed. That was what he meant me to do, of course. I realised that what he said was nothing but the truth; I stopped being clever about it. I accepted it. That was the pruning knife, Caiaphas, and now I have grown a new branch out of the old wood. And it will bear fruit."

"Well, well," said Caiaphas, "we all have these experiences from time to time. It does great credit to you, Nicodemus." He motioned to the servant to come over: "A little hot wine? It is a cold night."

"Do you suppose I would drink with you?" said Nicodemus.

"Probably I am not pious enough," said Caiaphas, and smiled a little.

"On the contrary. You are very pious towards—Cæsar."

"You think so, do you?" said Caiaphas with a growl in his voice. "One day, my friend, I will give you a lesson in politics."

Joseph of Arimathæa was trying to keep calm. Even if a shot went home, as that one had done on the High Priest, it would not help in the long run. He said: "I wonder if you see the situation correctly. Whatever Jesus may be, he has followers among the pilgrims, and others. In places you do not, perhaps, suspect. When they find out what you are doing—"

"I am aware of that, Joseph, my friend," said Caiaphas. "You will find it will not work out that way."

"But it is not only the Galileans. Perhaps it has not struck you, Caiaphas, but there is something about this prophet . . ."

"Do you believe he is, in all truth, Messiah?"

Joseph of Arimathæa hesitated. Nicodemus said: "Yes. I think he is." Then Joseph said: "So do I."

"Extraordinary!" said Caiaphas. "Educated men like yourselves!"

"We have been with him," Nicodemus said. "And I warn you, Caiaphas, if you murder the Messiah who is to save Israel there will be no forgiveness for you, either now or hereafter."

"I find myself doubtful about the hereafter," said Caiaphas. "My relation with the Lord our God and with Israel is here and now. My responsibility is here and now. I believe I am doing my best for Israel and for the God of Israel and for the Temple of Jerusalem our mother, by the action I am taking against someone who may make terrible trouble—worse, even, than we have already had—with the occupying power, which could crush all of us and defile our Temple. God knows they are near enough. One can scarcely move in the Temple without the thought of them staring down from the Antonia. Waiting to strike!"

"You have no doubts about what your prisoner is?"

"None," said Caiaphas, and shook his head and smiled.

The other two looked at one another. At last Joseph said: "Do you intend to kill him?"

"You will realise," said Caiaphas, "that our own powers are limited over a capital charge. And besides, it is almost Passover."

"What do you intend, then?" But Caiaphas did not answer that.

Finally Joseph asked: "Can we see the prisoner?"

"I am afraid not," said Caiaphas.

Nicodemus turned on his heel. "Come!" he said to Joseph, and with no goodbye to their host they walked out, heavy with anger and foreboding. Behind them Caiaphas turned again to his own party, which was going to do what he knew was best for Israel and for themselves.

     .   .   .   .   .

There was a little grey light beginning to come in the outer court, but it was still dark under the colonnade where John was waiting. "What did they say?" he asked. "Is there any hope?"

"I believe Caiaphas has the worst possible intentions towards his prisoner," said Nicodemus. "I also believe Jesus is the One foretold. If he is that, surely he will not stay in bonds, but rather show himself. . . ." His voice faltered, for he did not clearly see what he meant.

"He said he had to fulfil the prophecies," said John, "and they are mostly of pain and death and violence. The glory is afterwards."

"You think he means to die—and be lost to us?"

"I am not even sure if he can help it now," said John. And then: "Let me try to tell you about his powers of healing. They can only be used on those who ask it, either by speech or by touch or look. He would not—perhaps could not—heal one unwilling to be healed. There must somehow be a bond of love and faith as there was so strongly between him and Lazarus of Bethany. In the same way, if he has given up his own body, deliberately, to torture and death, can he save it? I do not think so."

They moved out into the half light of the street; there was no one about. The two older men were perplexed and uncertain, but young John had brought violently into his own mind the bodily shape of the Jesus whom he had been following for a year now, having given up all that most people would call the good things of life in order to do so. The body of Jesus of Nazareth which he had tried to spare from overwork and lack of sleep and stupid questions. There was a certain movement of the hands, a narrowing of eyes against the sun, dark eyes like a spring between great rocks. How in one's thought or love or any kind of reality can one separate a man from his body?

"Ought the pilgrims to be told?" asked Nicodemus uneasily.

"The Jerusalem mob?" said Joseph of Arimathæa. He thought no better of them than the rest of the priests did. Yet now perhaps they should be used.

"They will have been told," said John, "by the fishermen. Rocky—that is, Simon bar Jonas—is down there. Perhaps his cousins. I'm not sure where the others have got to; they were scared. But they may be there too. Somewhere in the Ophel and talking to people. I hope they have had the courage to do it!"

"That might mean—rioting," said Joseph.

"Yes," said John. "They'll do more than talk. You know, perhaps, that his mother and aunt are there, and one or two of his brothers."

"On his account?" asked Joseph.

"In a sense. They have been very critical, most of all lately. They had hoped he would be—oh, somehow different.

What they wanted themselves. What he wanted was too difficult for them."

"I remember his mother was known as a patriot," Nicodemus said, slowly, remembering. "A beautiful, strange girl, who made up songs. They are a wild, fierce people, those Galileans, never out of trouble. And giving it to others. Was it her grandfather who was out with the rebels in old Herod's time? Yes, I think he may even have been one of the men who held out in the Gorge of Pigeons. Terrible stories! And Mary's son will have heard them all from his mother."

"It was those stories, I think, and a horror of this world of killing and burning, of rape and screaming and the smell of blood, that sent James, the next son, into the Essenes. Away from it all."

"But Jesus took it differently."

"Yes," said John, "Jesus took it differently. He was going to change it into a world of love. For some of us—he did change it. Once you see how it could be, there is no possibility of living in any other way." He turned and looked back at the dark mass of the house against the greying sky. "I wonder where, in all that, he is."

.   .   .   .   .

If they had known, if they had been able to come near, they would yet have been kept separate by their own pity and anger and grasping love. These did not, any longer, properly apply to the prisoner. Cold, and bruises, and the stiffness of tied hands, are only momentarily noticeable to one who has disciplined the body, who has beaten down the threshold of pleasure and pain and wanting things, which stands between the individual and that eternity of which many people get glimpses but only a few the full experience. And this experience can never be passed on since there are no words for it. Stories and images are made about it, but carry no conviction to those who have not, themselves, seen what lies below them.

So he was thinking, with a love which no longer grasped at or tried to change them, about the twelve, one by one, separating out their minds and the amount of their understanding. He knew for certain that they did not understand yet; but later on it might come. That was something which must be left, to the Will, to be brought out. Or not. Even to the last, there was a deep and cloudy stupidity among the three fishermen, shot through by those curious flashes of intuition, lightning through clouds, so that they might yet—might yet be the builders of the Kingdom which he must die to bring about. Since no other price was high enough. Rocky, dear Rocky, Stormy and Flash. How could I think they would understand I had to die?

Judas perhaps saw that, Judas who kissed me at the last, to show that it was all on purpose, out of love. But am I even sure he knew what he was doing . . . that it was what I wanted . . . the step over the precipice that no man can take for himself? Bidden to go, with love. Judas must have lied to the Sadducees, perhaps taken money to make it seem credible. Would the rest ever understand that?

And then, violently, he wished it were all over, and he himself, not having made a mistake, having fulfilled all prophecies and accepted all sufferings, safe in the arms of eternity, like a father's arms.

Six

THE Old Man was in a filthy temper, and Hector was being very careful. He had heard a squealing in the night, perhaps the new girl. A pity if she was not satisfactory. It meant trouble all round. She had been well paid, too. And now there was this deputation of priests coming over with a prisoner, presumably the one the centurion had been talking about. It was curious how upset Esdras had been. The message had come over to the Residence just about dawn. Hector had left it to the soldiers to wake their Commander-in-Chief; the Old Man wasn't likely to lay one of *them* out. He had gone over to the Antonia fortress swearing like a butcher all the way, and Hector had followed with his heart in his mouth. He waited in the corner of the room with his tablets smooth and his stylus sharpened.

The Procurator walked over to the door, twitched away the curtain, frowned at what he saw, belched deliberately, and then spoke, more or less at Hector since there was nobody else there. "Bloody Jews," he said. He was a big dark man with crisp black hair, curling a little; it was the same on his chest and thighs. His mouth was large and his teeth in first-class order; he could tackle a steak with no bother. He was all togged up with quite a bit of gold on chest and arms, more than he would have worn in Rome. But then, this wasn't Rome.

Hector put himself into a bright, receptive attitude, almost feminine. His lips murmured a muted "Yes?"

"They think I can't see through them," said the Procurator, "but they're wrong. They want to make trouble the whole cursed time. First of all it's between me and the Fox. Not that I'd lose any sleep if young Herod went the same way as the rest of his family. But it's damned awkward. For all I know, they're going to Rome behind my back. Complaining. Saying they want a Senator instead of me. Yes, that's what they're after, some high-minded old buffer who'll let them get off with things. But I've got my friends there too. They won't get off with it. But what the devil do they want to bother me with now?"

Suddenly he snapped at Hector: "Here, you, go on down and tell them to come along to the judgment hall! Look sharp. And give that fat fool Gaius a kick when you're passing!"

Hector dashed out, and gave a discreet knock and a quick word to Gaius Valerius Crispus, who was on the Procurator's staff, a respectable young man, prematurely bald, and very hard-working; he had a little paunch, but only the Procurator called him fat. It was this Gaius who, a few minutes later, came in to tell His Excellency that the Jews were refusing to come into the judgment hall, as it would make them ritually unclean, and this was the evening of their feast. This provoked some bad language from the Procurator, but Gaius was good at calming him down. One had to allow for a certain amount of this when dealing with non-Europeans. The Syrians were just as bad. And, for that matter, it was quite pleasant in the courtyard now that the sun was up.

By the time the Procurator had come down into the open paved court everything had been got ready for him at the double. There was a large chair, its arms ending in Imperial eagles, heavily gilt. As it was still early, it had been put into the sunny side where His Excellency could have the back of his neck pleasantly warmed by the early rays. His audience would face the rising sun, and him. There they were, that crowd of Sadducees, always pretending to be so loyal, although you couldn't trust them a yard. They just didn't have the same values, and they had the bloody cheek to prefer their own to the Imperial ones. A lot better, thought the Procurator, to be somewhere like Pannonia or Moesia or Galatia, where at least the loyal ones really tried to absorb Roman civilisation and didn't pretend they had any of their own. But those were senatorial provinces, kept for the Big Boys. He'd never get beyond the minor places. And no doubt, though she didn't say so, that stuck-up bitch Claudia held it against him!

Half a dozen of those caterpillars from the priests' council, wearing all their robes and charms and nonsense, came along in front, making these ridiculous oriental gestures. Pontius Pilate sat extremely still looking slightly past them. The Temple guards were bringing a prisoner along with them, a small chap he looked, but you couldn't tell by that. "Well," he said suddenly. "That the accused? What's the charge?"

It was meant to annoy them, and did. "If he had not been a criminal, Your Excellency," said Caiaphas, "we would not have troubled you."

"You've got plenty of laws of your own," said Pilate, "which you keep on talking about. Take this man off and judge him according to your own laws."

"It is not lawful for us to put any man to death," said Caiaphas, narrowing his eyes against the sun and watching for the effect.

"Oh. It's like that, is it?" He leant over the arm of his chair and whispered to Gaius: "They've got something against this chap. He probably said they were a lot of stinking old billy goats; which they are. They want to get rid of him. You'll see. And want me to do their dirty work." He said aloud and very coldly: "Well, what is the accusation?"

Caiaphas was not going to let himself be rattled by this Roman. "He is a very dangerous man," he said, "in spite of his looks. Your Excellency, we found that he had been going

round the province leading the people astray. He told them
not to give tribute to Cæsar, saying that he himself is
Christos the anointed one; that is to say, Your Excellency,
a king."

This went home. "Bring him into the judgment hall,"
said Pilate, turning his back on them. They could stay
outside. He would see this man himself. Of course, if he did
actually assert that he was a king, then there was only one
thing to do. It wouldn't be the first Jew he had crucified.

The judgment hall was in the centre of the building, to
the west of the paved courtyard of the fortress; there was
nothing fancy about it; the place was a military building, not
an Eastern palace. At the back he had a little private inner
room which could be used for occasional religious purposes,
isolated, almost a bit of Rome. The gods of his household
were kept and honoured there; he had preferred it that way,
rather than having them in the Residence, old Herod's
palace. Somehow, he had felt, they would never accept that
as their home. But the Antonia fortress was part of the
Empire. His judgment seat in the hall was plain and Roman.
"I don't want all those guards," said Pilate; "a couple will
do." He sat down on the seat with Gaius standing beside
him; Hector was taking notes and would act as interpreter.
The prisoner apparently spoke no Greek, and, naturally, the
Procurator could not be expected to know all the native
languages.

When the prisoner was brought in, the Procurator had a
good look at him; suddenly he found himself rather liking
the man. One liked a prisoner who wasn't afraid, who kept
his eyes level. He spoke to him in a friendly way. "Are you
the King of the Jews?" he said, hoping that the man would
say it was all a put-up job and he had said nothing of the
kind. If he did that, Pilate intended to let him go, even
perhaps to give him some money. That would put those
others in their place! Hector translated.

The prisoner, however, said something unexpected. "Are

you asking me this because you think I am," he said, "or is it just that someone has told you it is being said?"

"Quite the Socrates!" said Pontius Pilate when it had been translated, and laughed a little; the man could stand up for himself. He wouldn't mind having a bit of an argument with him. "Naturally I don't think you are," he said. "I'm not one of you Jews!" The prisoner regarded him with the same unfrightened regard; yes, there was something kingly about him if you put it that way. "Now, come," said Pilate, "your own people are accusing you. The chief priests have brought you here, so there must be something wrong. What have you done?"

The man looked puzzled. Perhaps he thought quite genuinely that he had done nothing wrong. Perhaps he thought that Roman justice was bound to make this clear. "What's all this about a kingdom?" asked the Procurator.

Then suddenly the prisoner let go. "My kingdom is not of this world," he said. "If my kingdom were of this world my subjects would have fought for me, and I would never have been taken prisoner. But the Kingdom has nothing to do with this world of here and now." Hector translated this with some hesitation; it would not quite go word for word.

"What do you make of that?" Pilate said to Gaius.

"A mystic, sir; not a case for us at all."

"You really think so?"

"I've heard people use that kind of language—in some of the Egyptian Mysteries, for instance. He is probably quite harmless."

"He keeps on about kingdoms, though. And there was that matter of the tribute. Can't have anything interfering with that." He turned to the prisoner: "Now, you, stop talking in riddles. Are you or are you not a king?"

The prisoner said: "It is you yourself who talk about my being a king." He went on speaking, with the translator doing his best, but Pilate found it quite impossible to try to follow him; a lot of words you couldn't make head or tail of.

It only remained impressive that, although his hands were tied and although he looked like quite a poor man, to judge by his clothes and his untrimmed hair and beard, he spoke in this oddly authoritative way. "I came into the world for this alone," he said, "to bear witness to the truth. Every one that is of the truth hears my voice."

What can be made of that, except to say that the man may be a little mad but has the look of a good man? No reason, anyhow, why he should be allowed to be murdered by these miserable Sadducees. "What's truth, anyhow?" Pilate said, and walked out to the courtyard.

They were waiting there; in fact there were more of them now, waiting to hear that he was going to do what they wanted. He stood on the step until they quieted; then he said: "This man is not guilty of any criminal offence. I propose to discharge him."

What a row, all yelling at once, saying he was a trouble maker, guilty of sedition, blasphemy, they would send to Rome and tell Cæsar . . . ! The Procurator was not doing his duty! In the middle of it all someone was shouting: "The man has been preaching rebellion all through Judæa beginning from Galilee to here!" Listening, Gaius whispered: "There's your get-out, sir—the man's a Galilean."

Pilate shouted for silence, then demanded to know if this man was a Galilean. Yes, they said, that was so; a rebel from a rebel centre, that would show the kind he was! "Very well," said Pilate, "I shall send him to the Tetrarch; the man is in his jurisdiction." He grinned down at the crowd: "Under my own guards." He turned to Gaius: "That was bright of you, old cock. Lucky that Herod is in Jerusalem. By the way, did we ever get the man's name?"

Gaius did not know, but fortunately Hector had it down on his tablets: "Jesus bar Joseph, sir; common names, both of them."

The prisoner was taken out, to be marched over to Herod's palace; the accusers went off after him; Pontius

Pilate asked for a drink. The centurion at the gate watched them go by, with some distaste. "That's the one who was accused of sedition," he said, "but he doesn't look a bad type to me."

His older friend said: "He's the same one who's been going about doing cures. I wonder how he works it?"

"Some people have the gift," said the centurion. "They do it at the temple of Æsculapius."

"Ah yes, but that's knowledge," said the other man. "This chap's only a Jew."

.　　.　　.　　.　　.

Lady Claudia had not got to sleep again until near dawn, and still it seemed like an uneasy sleep. She must be dreaming, thought Barsiné, away in that terrible world where anything may happen, where a virtuous woman is not safe from demons. Could it be this shouting they could just hear in the street outside which had come through to her, menacing and horrible? In a while she woke, but would not tell Barsiné her dreams, except to say that she thought some wrong thing was being done, somewhere near at hand. But the world is so full of wrong, how could anyone try to put it right? A lady should not even think about it. To do so might take away from her the special quality which was most valued in her. Surely that must be so?

In the distance there was some singing now, women's voices in a kind of chant, not, somehow, the same kind that one heard so often round the Temple of Jerusalem. Barsiné was listening too, and smiling. "What is it?" Lady Claudia asked.

Barsiné looked a tiny bit startled: "It is the Adonis, my lady," she said; "they go out into the fields and find the blood drops——"

"What are you talking about, child?"

"The—the flowers of Adonis, my lady. . . ."

"Oh yes, the little red ones. I've heard about this. They

are mourning the poor Adonis, are they? But surely Jewish
women would not do that?"

"No," said Barsiné, "but in Jerusalem there are so many,
many kinds of people. It is the middle of the world, and my
lady lives there! But these ones, they say they must mourn
the Adonis or he will not live again. And then the corn will
not spring."

"I think I like the sounds," said Lady Claudia almost to
herself; she sat for a while in front of her mirror looking at
herself intently, rubbing at a wrinkle here or there that came
in spite of anything she did. Unfair, only to have one life.
She was only half dressed when another of the slaves came in
to say that Madame Joanna, the wife of Chuza, Herod's
treasurer, was waiting, and hoped, although it was so early,
that she might see her. "Yes, indeed!" said Claudia, "the
very one I want to see. Just make me presentable, Barsiné—
no, don't bother about my curls. That head scarf. The
sandals with the ivory clasps, that's right. And, oh dear,
she won't be fussy about food, will she? Fruit would be safe,
anyhow. Bring some of the preserved plums and some nice
raisins and nuts!"

Joanna, the wife of Chuza, was not certain whether she
could achieve anything or whether this Roman lady only
wanted to see her out of curiosity. The small politenesses, at
any rate, had to be gone through. Joanna was middle-aged
and grey-haired now; she had duly borne a brood of sons
and brought most of them up; her daughters were safely
married. She had been able to begin to think a little beyond
the close circle of home. But what she thought of had not yet
included the occupying power. Actually it was Claudia who
brought the subject up.

"I wish you would tell me," she said, "something about
this new prophet, Jesus of Nazareth."

Joanna the wife of Chuza took a deep breath. Her own
dress was heavily embroidered in threads of bullion, and she
wore many necklaces which tinkled a little as she moved.

5—BYK

Chuza's wife could do no otherwise. "Why do you want to know, Lady Claudia?" she asked. They were talking in Greek, the common language of the Mediterranean, which most educated people knew, though it was far from the Greek of Plato.

"Because—" said Claudia, "because I feel—oh, he may have some secret I have been looking for. I dreamt about him all last night."

"You know he has been arrested?"

"Arrested . . . no, I did not know. On what charge?"

"Sedition, perhaps. Let me tell you how it came about and you shall judge him. He has had the direct experience of God. Do you know what I mean, Lady Claudia?"

"I am not sure," she said, "unless you tell me where it led."

"It led him to the certainty that God is his father."

"In what sense?"

"In two senses. First, for us in Judæa he is God's son, the Son of Man whom we have been waiting for all these long generations, who will at last rescue us."

"Rescue you! From—" Claudia flushed and spoke with a certain hardness—"from the Empire?"

"That is not in question. It is from ourselves, from the hardness of our hearts, from our knowing the Law and the Commandments and yet letting our brothers and sisters starve. From—cruelty of all sorts. Not even being aware that things are wrong."

"I see. And the other sense?"

"The other sense is that God is the father of all kinds of life: of plants creeping up between two stones in the desert, of wild birds and little worms and flies, and dogs covered with sores. And that in God's sight one life is as valuable as another. The slave with his master. The condemned with his judge."

"Yes, that might be sedition in any State if it was carried

through to the end. Do you believe in this, Madame Joanna?"

She said slowly: "I believe it. If I were free I would carry it out. As you see—" she touched the necklaces on her broad bosom—"though it is a kind bondage, I am not free."

"No," said Claudia, "we are none of us free. No woman. And if we were all equal together . . ."

"In a state of love. Regarding the not-self as dearer than the self. That is what Jesus of Nazareth calls the Kingdom. But it is not a kingdom against—Rome or the tetrarchy. They do not, in a sense, exist. Am I shocking you, Lady Claudia?"

"No. No, I can see it has its—attraction. To be able to see that world so clearly. The world of all who have ever had that vision. There have been others, you know, Madame Joanna, and outside your country. The Garden that Epicurus dreamt of. Agis. Cleomenes. When I was a girl I used sometimes to wonder whether, if I had been alive then—— Oh, I would so much like to meet this prophet of yours! Is it possible?"

"But I told you——"

"He has been arrested. Yes. By us?"

"No. By the Sadducees. You see, because Jesus of Nazareth is specially God's son, and in full understanding, he can use his Father's power for good over all life."

"It's true, then, about the healing?"

"Quite true. Being what he is, nothing else makes sense. But those who have always had power and can see nothing beyond power, cannot bear knowing there is a greater power than theirs. They have to try to break it. That is what is happening now."

"I wonder if the case is likely to come before my husband?"

"If it does, will you . . ."

Claudia looked away, wondering what effect anything she might say would have. "I will try," she said.

Seven

IN the little room, sharp spears of sunlight had darted themselves through the cracks in the shutter. The young Mary lay asleep on the floor; her face was very white and she stirred in her sleep. The older Mary took one of the woollen wraps that still smelt of sheep, and laid it over her gently. "Poor child," she said, "she isn't used to this. And it may be a hard day yet." Doing this with tenderness, there was the remains of an old beauty and grace about her.

The other old woman, her cousin Salome, was kneeling beside the hearth, blowing up the embers. She was the mother of Stormy and Flash, the two Zebedee boys. She turned her head: "None of us are used to it, Mary, and that's a fact. I had two servant girls at home. Not that they were much use unless I was always on top of them, and what I say is, one can do a thing oneself in half the time it takes to tell another woman." She put on some dry thorn sticks and the fire crackled up. "Give me the flour, Mary, and an egg. I'll make some pancakes. They'll want something when they get back. . . ." She had half opened the shutter and then found a small metal plate and put it to heat over the fire. She kept on talking, half to herself: "My boys were always good providers. Perhaps they'll go back to the fishing now, help their poor father. My James's Hannah is fair heart-broken. He never sends her a word, not so much as a piece of ribbon. I wish we were well out of here. This room, I don't like it. And me thinking maybe it was all true about the kingdom and that the boys would get something out of it."

Mary turned round suddenly: "It *is* true," she said, "but not the way you mean, Salome!"

"So you're saying that now, are you, dear?" Salome said with a certain malice. This woman's son had pulled her sons after him. Now he was probably going to be executed as some kind of rebel. So long as he didn't take her sons with him there.

The young Mary slept on, and the old Mary leant forward, watching the new bright sunlight creep across the earth floor, showing up all the cracks and twigs and crumbs. "I always knew my son would be the Chosen One," she said. "I knew from the time I was a girl that I had it in me to bear him! Don't you remember what I used to say?"

"All those songs," Salome said indifferently.

"But I didn't know how it would take him. He was such a clever boy. And then, after he'd gone off to the Jordan and John had made him reborn—well, he seemed to change. I couldn't understand him any more. He did all these things. Oh I do so remember that wedding at Cana: how proud I was! But it took something out of him all the time. And I couldn't do anything to help. I couldn't give him back his strength any more, as I could when he was a child. I used to get angry when he turned to other people the same way he used to turn to me. It's terrible when a boy grows away from you although you love him so much. And I'd all the others to bring up after their poor father died." Salome was not listening now; she had mixed the pancakes and kept holding her palm out to the metal plate to see if it was hot enough.

The young Mary turned and muttered, and the old Mary patted her shoulder as though she had been a child, still talking, half to herself: "Poor lamb, she's worn herself out. Loving him though she doesn't know it, and giving up everything. We think ourselves above this, Salome, because we had nice little houses and a bit of land, and our Jerusalem cousins haven't done so well and only have this one room and the shed, though they always ask us for Passover."

"Because of what we bring," Salome snapped.

"No, it's not. We'd be welcome without the lamb and the chickens and your dried fish and the oil and flour! I can feel that if you can't. But this one—you didn't see her father's house at Magdala, but I did. Quite a little palace, more doors than you could count round a courtyard with pot herbs growing in rows, and roses. She never did a stroke of work, not real work. Of course, she had these devils, poor child, and if she hadn't been a rich man's daughter she might have come to a bad end, fallen into a fire or been sent out to beg—men always want to look at a girl with devils throwing herself about and then anything can happen. I was so glad when he cured her, so proud. Every time he did a thing like that I believed in him again, though I did think he was saying dangerous things. Against the rules. Dangerous. . . ." Her face darkened with foreboding. "I wish I knew where they'd all gone!"

"Gone to look for arms and rouse up the pilgrims and then fight and get themselves killed," said Salome grimly. "I'm glad my own boys had more sense. That Rocky!"

"And then she gave up everything to follow him. That home and a lovely wedding all being got ready for her. Silk dresses. But he always makes people give up everything. If they really care. Or he really cares for them. Young John Priest was the same. That giving up was what he meant by the Kingdom. Giving up by your own free choice."

"I never could see why he called it the Kingdom if he didn't mean—power and glory and that," said Salome, turning over the pancakes.

"That was his name for what happened when people were at peace because they didn't want to own things. Or own one another. I used to understand for a bit. And then it slipped away."

Suddenly the young Mary woke, sat straight up, looked

about her. "Oh, Mother," she said, "you've been to the well! And swept the room and everything! How could I have been so selfish!"

"You were tired out, child. I wanted you to sleep."

"Yes, I was tired. Is there any news?" Mary shook her head. "At least there is no sentence yet?"

"We know nothing," said the older Mary. "My dear, we must wait."

Then the door burst open, letting in more light, and a young man came in, seeming to fill the room with life and energy: John, nicknamed Flash for his sudden bursts of anger, the younger son of Zebedee and Salome. He was a tall, tough-looking boy, with the tanned arms and face of a fisherman. His mother burst out at him: "I thought you'd had sense enough to go home! What are you doing here?"

"I'd sense enough to pick myself out of a thorn bush the other side of Kedron and come back. I've seen John Priest. We'll need to try and rouse the Quarter. But nobody knows just what they've done with him."

"Where's your brother?" asked Salome.

"Don't know. We got scattered. Give me something to eat." He snatched up a pancake and crammed it into his mouth. "Worst of it is, they've lost heart a bit here, after the Tower affair last year. Got it into their heads that the head ones are always going to win. I heard there was a chap called Malachi who had some guts—if we could get hold of him . . ."

"He is helping," said young Mary in a very low voice. "I—he spoke to me."

"Good for you, Miss Mary!" said Flash. "I'll go and find them—we must make a plan——"

"Son," said the old Mary suddenly, laying a hand on his sleeve, "there was a saying of my son Jesus that is coming back to me. He said he would be taken and killed and then he would rise again. When they told me he had said that, I thought he was dreaming—I thought of him as one thinks of a boy. It is difficult to bear a child and then he grows up and is a man, and far from you. It is harder yet if he grows up to be the Messiah. And now it begins to seem to me that he meant to die in the flesh, in this flesh that I made and fed with my milk and washed and combed—" now there was a sob coming into her voice—"so that afterwards he may come back in glory—and he will have no more body to suffer with but only—only . . ." She looked up at the young man. "How could my son become God?"

The fisherman was looking terribly troubled. At last he said: "There was a thing happened, and he told us not to tell. But maybe I should tell you now. It was more than a year ago. We were high up among the mists, me and Stormy and Rocky, following him among the rocks and stones. And there was shining and appearances. We thought he was walking with the prophets themselves and it was scaring. And there was a voice . . . . But he said we were to tell nobody till the Son of Man was risen from the dead. And we didn't know— we wondered what he could mean—and now—now if he means to die . . ."

"What was the voice you heard?" said Mary. "What did it say?"

"It seemed," said the young man, "like the voice of the Lord God and it said—it said He was pleased——"

"With my son?"

"With His son."

"So—it may be that what is happening is—intended," said Mary, half to herself.

From behind her, Salome said to her son: "If that's true, then it means one thing for you today: don't meddle. What's to be must take its course."

Flash threw up his hand: "If it is so, it is in God's hand, but that does not mean that I'm not going to do my duty by my master and teacher the way I see it!" And suddenly he turned and went out of the room again.

"He's a fine boy, your Flash," Mary said to her cousin. "One of the best." And then: "If only I knew they weren't hurting my boy."

.   .   .   .   .

They could hear noises at some distance in the Quarter, but impossible to say what it was. Young Mary offered to go and see, but the older ones thought it best to stay in the house. They would know soon enough. After a while a woman neighbour came in, to tell them that there was a great to-do on, and some were all for an attack, but others remembered this time a year ago; there'd been the fighting at the Tower and the soldiers getting the best of it—always would, they had the real weapons—and poor Bar Rabban still in prison, the Lord be with him. So the men were arguing and shouting about it and some of them had got hold of some swords and were swinging them around, and someone had made up a song against the Sadducees and anyone who was dirty enough to take Roman citizenship and wear the Roman stripes and do any kind of dirt for the Romans— oh, it was a real hot song and a lot had taken it up. . . .

She was still talking when Malachi bar Joses came in; he was wearing a leather coat with metal shoulder guards and a metal collar, practical enough for street fighting, and he had what looked like a good sword at his belt, a sword and a dagger. He said: "They are trying to have him condemned to death. They took him to the Roman, but it seems he wouldn't do it. Now he's been taken to Herod; being a Galilean. We didn't get word of it at first. And it's all up in their part of the city. Behind their walls. We don't see yet how to work it. But we will."

"And—and rescue him?" young Mary said.

"That's it, girl. And after that . . ." He went over and caught her by the elbows, squeezed her up against him and sucked at her half-open mouth, and then was gone, leaving the girl in scalding, choking tears and her face scarlet.

"So that's your fancy, is it!" Salome said. "I wonder what your poor father would say——"

"Hush!" said her cousin, "can't you see—child, what are you doing? Did you make him a promise?"

"If—if he saves—the Son . . ."

"That shows a great love," said Mary gravely, "a very great love."

"A great excuse!" said her cousin, "didn't you see——"

"No!" said the young girl, her hand up to scratch the older woman's face open. Then, slowly she let it fall. "Forgive me," she said, "you—didn't understand." She dropped back against the wall and pressed her hot face against the cool mud plaster, trying to scrape the touch and smell out of her mouth, trying to forget what she had felt of him as he pulled her to him.

"I understand," said the older Mary, at her shoulder; "perhaps I would have promised the same, if my body had been worth yours. But—child, we must be sure what we are doing, as I was sure once. When he was safe in my womb. But I am not sure any longer." Then she said: "Yesterday he kept Passover, not with me and his brothers, as would have been his place as the eldest, the head of our family now that his father is dead, but with those twelve whom he called to follow him. All the time I was thinking about him; during the breaking of the bread and the drinking of the wine. We had brought it on ourselves. We had separated ourselves from him, we had not trusted him. Our Passover was lonely for me, and perhaps for his brothers, without him. But our suffering may yet be together."

Eight

(7 to 8 a.m.)

IN the Jerusalem household of Herod the Tetrarch, great preparations for the Passover were going on. Herod Antipas always came up to Jerusalem for the occasion, or indeed whenever any sufficient excuse presented itself. It was at least livelier than his own tetrarchy; how boring Galilee could be! Nothing new. Always grumble, grumble, and the synagogues used for making speeches against him and his family. Passover in Jerusalem did at least mean pilgrims from Asia Minor and Greece and Italy, who might have new things to sell or new ideas to discuss. Both were welcome.

Herod Antipas being, like the Sadducees, on the side of the State, was going to keep Passover that evening in spite of Sabbath. So there was a great scrubbing and cleaning and the tables to be prepared with silver and gold, though the food would be the same in the old Hasmonean Palace as in some poor house in the Ophel. Herod himself found the Passover rather a bore. Politically, of course, he was a devout Israelite, but it went no farther back than his grandfather, father of the great Idumean Herod, who had thought conversion advisable with this exceedingly difficult kingdom to cope with. So at the back of his mind Herod Antipas held the possibility of other gods.

Meanwhile he was thinking of spending the morning in the small garden in the centre of his town house, which was the old Hasmonean Palace. It was here that he kept his choice menagerie with young leopards, peacocks and singing birds, an ostrich, several gazelles, some amusing crocodiles in the marble pond, and various dwarfs, male and

67

female, who would tumble and dance or make love whenever it pleased him. It was pleasant to be rich and powerful, to have ownership of an absolute and terrible kind, to wear gold and silk and fine furs and eat and drink whatever you liked. But it would have been very much pleasanter to be a real king with no Rome ready and willing to turn you out if you took a wrong step and banish you to the back of beyond, and no brother Philip with a tetrarchy as good or better.

He could not, for example, enjoy the genuine excitements of war, only the less amusing pleasures of politics. He couldn't even go in for building on a satisfactory scale, or the Romans would get suspicious. The Jerusalem priesthood might get suspicious too, and start setting the people even more against him than they were already. If only he had been a real ruler like his father, what a pleasure it would have been to get hold of Caiaphas and—oh well, it was out of the question. He had to put up with him and exchange politenesses. And so it went. A shame for a ruler of the house of Herod to be so thwarted! No war, no real magnificence. Women became a bore. Boys became a bore. Hunting, even, had a sameness after a time. So when, on a bright and sunny morning, word came to him that the new prophet had been caught and was being sent over to him to be examined, he couldn't have given himself a greater treat. "We shall see some first-class magic," he said to the two girls who were clinging on to him, and hurried back inside the palace. It was a compliment, too, that the Procurator had sent the man over; perhaps he was trying to be friendly, if so why and against whom? That one would want thinking over.

He was sitting on his smaller throne when the guards brought in the prisoner. The two current girls were curling round his feet and as many of his court as could get in were waiting to see the fun. Chuza, the treasurer, was there of course: a proud old boy who took his duties very seriously and wasn't always sympathetic with the way his master liked to spend the money. But loyal to the dynasty; oh yes, no fault to find there.

The old Hasmonean throne was well cushioned and elegantly canopied in a more elaborate taste than the Procurator's official chair, and Herod Antipas himself affected more jewels and longer robes, and shoes with proud curling toes instead of the plain Roman sandal. He had a wine-bearer standing just beside the throne. You never knew, this might develop into quite a party. There were several monkeys tied to the pillars of the canopy by little gilt chains, some wearing skirts or long embroidered trousers. It was always a good joke to watch them scratch and bite one another or themselves under these mock humanities.

"Well now," said Herod, "here's someone I've been wanting to see for a long, long time. You know," he said, beckoning them to bring the prisoner close up to him, "you're my subject, but you never came to do me homage. That was bad of you, but perhaps I shan't punish you. Perhaps. You called me the Fox, didn't you? But this Fox won't bite you, not if you're sensible." He tried to see what effect he was having. It ought to have scared the prisoner a little, made him anxious to please. Herod Antipas knew that he was most alarming when he was most apparently amiable.

But he couldn't tell this time. "Loose him!" he said to the guards. "He won't run away. No, he won't run away from his lawful sovereign, will he?" Then, as they were slow to do it he shouted at them: "Look sharp there! Are you afraid he'll turn you into pigs?" And to the prisoner: "You could do that easily, couldn't you? And I wouldn't mind if you did. A few guards one way or another, who cares? They hurt you, didn't they? Pulled you about? Go on—turn them into something!"

Considerable uneasiness among the guards, but not a word, not a movement from the prisoner. Although his arms were now free he barely moved them. This was irritating for the Tetrarch. He was not used to having to wait. The gauze-trousered cuties were watching him sideways from under their drooped eye-lids. His friends were watching, standing proud and silent in a glitter of gold. Old Chuza, the treasurer, gulped and took a step towards him, was going to say something. The Tetrarch glared at him, then back at the prisoner.

"Show me something," said Herod. "I want to see you do things. Raise a devil for me!"

Still nothing.

"You've got the names of Power, I know you have. Use them. Make a circle! Write the Name! Make me a woman! Bring the Queen of Sheba!"

Nothing.

"Is it that there are too many people here? Shall we go to another room? You and me—alone? Will that do? Shall I send the others away? Do you want a sacrifice?" A sacrifice —perhaps that was it. He stared at the face so close to him but got no response at all. "Where is your power from? Some say you talk to Moses and the old prophets. Have you sold yourself to the Evil One? I think you have!" He looked round. Here and there people were tittering, partly at the prisoner but partly at him, Herod the Tetrarch, who couldn't deal with this prisoner. His voice became less pleasant. "Don't pretend. I know you are a magician. I know you have the Names. Make manna come down. I shall be angry if you don't show me something. You won't like it if I'm angry. Give him a look at the whips!" The guards brought them eagerly. "There, you see. Now show me something."

But it was as though the prisoner had heard nothing.

Suddenly the Tetrarch seized on one of the monkeys, snapping its chain, and threw it hard down on to the marble so that its back was broken. He caught up the wriggling, jerking thing and threw it at the prisoner: "Cure that, make it whole!"

Still nothing, only that the prisoner seemed to shiver a

little as though indeed he had seen and felt what had been done. The monkey's twitchings became feebler and died out. Its eyes filmed over. Its horrible little skirt dropped over a dribble of blood. Herod was half whispering now: "Make it come alive! As you did Lazarus at Bethany. You see, I know everything. Do what I say!" Suddenly his temper went, and he threw a cup of wine at the prisoner who wouldn't speak. It bounced off him and rattled across the marble floor.

"All right!" said Herod. "What's the accusation?" And he glared at the priests. How much he disliked these Sadducees who had got in with Rome, got themselves made citizens, even went to Rome; but if the prisoner wasn't going to play his game, then let him get what was coming!

But this accusation of theirs that the new prophet had set himself up as a king against Cæsar was utter nonsense. Anyone could see that, anyone but a fool of a Sadducee. There was nothing wrong with this particular Galilean except that he happened to be a stiff-necked peasant who couldn't see what was good for him. King indeed! Stopping the tribute indeed! Caiaphas was probably jealous because he'd never be able to do any magic if he lived to be a hundred.

But I'm going to have some fun, Herod thought to himself, glowering round from accusers to prisoner and back. He beckoned to one of his particular friends: "See what you can do to get something out of him."

His friends were not averse. The prisoner was one of these prophets, one of these virtuous ones who set themselves up to be better than the rest of the world, who despised rulers and powers. It would be amusing to take him down. Not, of course, to torture him, since he might be—well, someone special. And if he was, that gave one the extra thrill. Since he might retaliate! But he did not even do that.

Caiaphas looked away, a little sick. This was disgusting. Chuza the treasurer looked away. He knew that his wife, whose opinion he valued, since she was a good and wise

woman and had borne him sons, had a particular regard for
this man. He did not look forward to telling her what had
happened, but she was not someone who could be lied to.
The Roman guards shrugged their shoulders: so long as the
prisoner wasn't actually killed there was no harm done.
Herod and his cuties laughed and laughed. An Israelite
countryman, even if he is not one of the pure and dedicated,
does not like to be stripped, to have to hear what the women
are saying, to feel their defiling, nipping fingers. Can the
body, then, be not regarded at all? This body that is soon to
be left, with all its soiling and shame. But the body, like an
over-anxious wife, catches at the spirit, and drags it down to
make them one again.

Alternately there is complete acceptance of shame and
pain and mockery, the sliding spit in the face, the cut of the
whip, the sting of the nettles and the rope tight across thighs
and chest. In all these voices there was not one voice which
was fully human, which had in it the thing which could be
spoken to. Better, then, to be silent and let the prophecies
come about, as they had to; the sorrows and pains of the
Messiah.

Herod came and stood in front of him: "Are you sorry
now you didn't do what I wanted? Listen, get yourself out
of this, melt these ropes away and I'll believe in you. Say
the Name! Say the Name!" No use, and he took off his own
belt, quite slowly. It had a clasp made like golden lions'
claws. It was obvious what he was going to do and one of the
girls gave a little shriek of excitement. He brought down the
belt flat across the thin belly of the prisoner, with a jerk so
that the claws jagged blood out of him. "So much for not
speaking," he said.

That was over. The hot flush died out of the Tetrarch's
elegant, half-Arab face. In another, colder voice, he called
the guard. "Put his own clothes back on to him. That's right.
Now, take him back to His Excellency the Procurator and

tell him that I have examined the prisoner myself and find
that he is not guilty."

Caiaphas looked at his colleagues; this was not going
quite as it should. He had not wanted the prisoner to be
mocked and spat upon. He had only wanted to have him
killed. One of them said: "But if the Roman still will not
do it?"

"We shall have to insist that he does," Caiaphas said.

"How?"

"I think we shall have to make it plain that if there is any
temporising about this particular crime we will complain to
Tiberius Cæsar. Apparently Cæsar believes in his own
godhead! There are some other matters for complaint, as
you know, Eleazar, about which we have kept silent so far.
Our friend Pilate is not beyond reproach."

"There has been some bribery . . ."

"On a large scale, and I have witnesses. Also, there has
been some terrorising. In quarters which—were nothing to
do with Rome: should have been immune. In other
provinces, Syria for instance, this has not happened; there
has been another type of Governor. It should not have
happened here. Persons have complained to me. The time
seems to have arrived to deal with that. There have been
other Procurators who had higher standards. I think I shall
have to get this into His Excellency's mind—at some point.
Find me a piece of parchment, will you?"

Nine

(*8 to 9 a.m.*)

IT hadn't been too easy to get into the rich part of the city without being suspected. They'd come in twos and threes, wearing old coats over anything else they might have. Some of them had snatched up a cabbage or a few green almonds or a flat loaf, anything to look as if they were there on business. And it was scaring, after the twisty streets and mud walls of their own quarter, the doorways where they could dodge, the known roof-top ways and the shutters that would open for a man in a hurry, to have these great hewn stone walls, high and squared, with only maybe a high-up window, barred like a prison. There was a paved edge to the road too, so you wouldn't get your feet in the honest mud and dust. Enough to make a man feel—queer.

And yet Stormy knew, oh he knew in his bones that they'd get the Son away. Back from the rich who'd trapped him but were going to be laid low now. As it had been said by the prophets! He and Twin waited at a corner where they could see, but not seem to be watching. And it was the same at all the other corners. And that lot sitting on the edge of the pavement, letting on they were playing a dice game—yes, it's our lot, he thought, and then whispered to his friend: "Didn't you get a sword, Twin?"

"I'm not safe with a sword, and that's a fact," said Twin. "I'd cut my own nose off. Or yours, Stormy. Or his, so help me. But I've got plenty of stones. That chap Malachi says the soldiers don't like stones."

"Well, see you don't hit *him*."

"He'll be in the middle of them, won't he?"

74

"We don't know. We've got to trust it'll work out right. And so it will! If only we knew what they're doing to him. In there."

The gates of the Hasmonean Palace remained shut, great cedar planks sheathed with heavy bronze. The walls were immensely strong. So do the rich guard themselves against the poor. They waited, and the sun grew hotter and the dust began to blow.

Malachi bar Joses counted up his forces. If only they'd had a bit more time! There were his own crowd who had some experience of street fighting, but not all of them had been willing to come for this. They were patriots, right enough, but they didn't see this Nazareth preacher as another Maccabee. He was beginning to wonder if they were right and he himself seeing it wrong, just because of that little sweet-mouthed piece he wanted and saw his way to get. They'd listened to this preacher, some of them, when he was talking in front of the Temple, but what he said didn't always have much meaning; what was the use of stories? An old-fashioned kind of way of working, you wanted more fire and life, something to make you hate and do something! Besides, he took the hecklers all wrong, couldn't tell which were serious and which were half friendly but having him on a bit. A real leader—oh, he must be able to handle all sorts! Someone like the other Jesus, Bar Rabban, who was in prison somewhere. If only they could get him back they'd make some headway against these Romans and Romanisers.

But Malachi thought, all the same, that this Jesus whom the fishermen followed would turn into a leader of their own kind, the kind they needed. A leader had to be able to see ahead; he had to see through the darkness and tangle round the head ones who were always doing something unexpected, tricking and tripping and using their power—unless you could get in under the guard. What Malachi wanted was to be a sword in the hand of a leader. He had been that for Bar Rabban. He wanted that most. And the other thing he wanted was to have this lady; a man like him didn't get the chance of a maidenhead more than once or twice in a lifetime, not like Herod in there taking his pick. She'd asked for it, going round with that Jesus and his lot. Why hadn't one of them taken the chance? Crazy—afraid to defile themselves with women. Afraid, that was all. He wasn't afraid, not if she screamed the house down; if she did he'd treat her rough. Slowly he flexed and straightened his right arm, admiring the muscle. Maybe he'd marry her later, might get something from her father—spin a yarn—but he couldn't wait for that. He'd go back to that room in the heat of the day, turn out the two old pussies and then—then—rough it would be. But this job had got to be done first.

Apart from his own crowd there were some of the man's own Galileans. The fishermen—they should be all right. He wasn't too sure of the others; pilgrims from the country, mostly, with every kind of crazy notion. They weren't used to this. Frightened of being in a city. Got lost, same as an animal might. Frightened of high walls and the twist and dark of a street. And then there was the brother Simon—worried sort of chap, always had to look after the family business—and one or two cousins, but not the brother they called Judge; a queer one that, didn't believe in the world. Didn't believe in Israel, only in the Lord God. But what was God anyway—apart from Israel? Didn't make sense.

They'd got maybe sixty or seventy, not all armed. A bit more time and it would have been hundreds. Pull it off and it would be thousands! They'd got to make the most of themselves against the professionals. Stones. After some thought he'd decided to leave a couple of dozen to come up afterwards, yelling and throwing things, so as to look as if the whole Quarter were attacking. That was the kind of thing Bar Rabban had been good at.

And still the gate didn't move. No sound from behind the walls, only somewhere hens, and a goat, and a woman singing at her work. We're doing right, said Rocky to himself,

we're doing right. I'll show I love him best. I'll make it so
that cock didn't crow!

It was John Priest who was most uneasy. He had to be
there with the others, once they'd made up their minds, but
somehow he knew this wasn't the way to do it. You might
get an ordinary prisoner back this way. But not the Son of
Man. If Caiaphas had come to a political decision, it wasn't
a small riot that would stop him; sooner or later they would
be back in the same place. And this—he looked round—
surely, surely, it was all against what had been taught? Love
one another, he had said; keep the Commandments. Resist
not evil. Turn the other cheek. Love your enemies. Be
perfect. Over and over, trying to get them to see.

But there had been other things. Stories of violence, and
if you tried to interpret them anything might be meant!
Rocky, Flash, the Twin, they are here out of love . . .
which has cast out fear. What else? Is my love, then,
smaller than theirs, he thought, with sudden pain; is it the
smallness of my love that makes me uncertain? Or do I
know better what love feeds on? Well, he will say himself,
if this comes off. He will say if he wants to go back into the
safe and lovely hills of Galilee. But if he had wanted that he
would never have come to Jerusalem. He knew—he knew
he was coming to his death!

Then, slowly, the gates were pushed outward and forward.
There was a sharp word of command that rang in the arch
of the gates, and the guard came through, a squad of Roman
soldiers armed with short stabbing swords and Temple
guards with spears. The gate shut to behind them. Inside
the ranks of guards, the prisoner. Behind them, a small
crowd, Caiaphas, Eleazar, more of the ones they hated! But
it was the sight of the foreigners above all, the filthy
idolatrous Romans, that sent the blood to their heads and
the yell into their throats. The moment the enemy got clear
of the gates so that they couldn't dodge back inside, the
fight started.

It had to be quick, to take the guards by surprise so that the whole thing would be over before they could get help, either from Herod's guard or from the Roman garrison. Make them think they'd got the whole people of Jerusalem against them—that was the essential. Nothing like a good volley of sharp stones to get a guard into a mess. Helmets knocked off and faces cut before they'd got their shields up. As for them, it wasn't as if they had anyone important to guard, just a wretched Galilean peasant who had been accused of some ridiculous crime and declared innocent! The sergeant-in-charge was all for letting him go—if only the man would make a break for it instead of just standing there. Better lose him than risk good Roman lives, and it seemed like they'd got the whole of this blasted town against them!

The Temple guards were a tougher nut to crack. They'd an idea this prisoner mattered, and Caiaphas was shouting at them to hold him. But these Galileans—there was the one who'd got in such a swipe the evening before when they'd picked up this false Messiah—a dangerous devil of a fanatic, swinging a great sword about! Spears aren't the best for close fighting and the stones kept on zipping in—here were some more men coming at them over the wall, yelling—it would be a real riot—this was the Bar Rabban gang—they'd bitten off more than they could chew. . . .

And then, among flying stones and bangs and slashes and curses and blood, the fishermen got through and picked up the prisoner and carried him off. They were making for a place they knew, where, by a back way and a roof, they could get over the dividing wall safe into the Ophel, their own Ophel, the old city of David!

"What's the damage?" The Roman sergeant was panting, straightening his helmet, feeling at his funnybone. An eye knocked out, fingers broken, half a dozen bleeding heads and two or three out for the count, lying on the edge of the pavement—dirty brutes of Jews, we'll get them yet! He looked round at the others; one of the Temple guards was doubled up over a knife wound that had got in under his armour, and two others had nasty flesh wounds. Caiaphas, with a cut over one eye that he didn't appear to notice, was giving orders furiously. Six of the Temple guards set off, rather half-heartedly, to track down the Galileans. But there was a rear action of stones thrown. They'd be sure to get the prisoner down into the Ophel, the tangle of dark streets where an official might get knifed by a hand he never saw— nothing to be done but burn out half the Quarter.

"You all right, Twin? What's the matter?"

"One of my stones. It hit a man in the eye. . . ."

"What about it? Only a Roman. I'd think no more than if he was a gaffed fish—we've got the Son, got him away from them!"

I wasn't afraid, Rocky thought, not for one moment, only that we might hurt *him* by mistake. I came at them like a bull—I've proved myself! And now. Now. We did it, we got him away; the Kingdom will come!

The man next him suddenly gasped and caught hold of his shoulder. "You hurt?" asked Rocky.

"Inside—somewhere," said Malachi. "I feel myself— bleeding away—got under my guard. . . ."

Rocky put an arm round him: "Shan't be long now, then we'll see to you."

But something was slowing them up. They were going for their own place, to the poor and the pilgrims who would welcome their King back from the Powers of Darkness. And then away, out of the net. But the Son had turned and was standing still and speaking to them, asking them what they thought they were doing and why. He looked very pale and there were little splashes of blood and dirt on his face. He began to say over the names of his own, catching their eyes and pulling them out from the rest. Flash, Stormy. He even smiled a little, so sure he was that those two would be in it! John, Rocky. "Where is Judas?" he asked.

"Judas!" said Rocky. "We hope in hell!" No, they didn't understand. Nor ever would.

The only answer to that was: "If he betrays the Son of Man with a kiss, you betray him with swords." He put out his hand and touched the wet blade. "Have you forgotten already what I told you?"

Suddenly Rocky dropped his sword as though it had turned into something foul in his hand. "Did we betray you?" he said, stumblingly. "Truly—master . . ."

"Until you know that my kingdom is not of this world, you will always betray me." He looked away from them, in deep trouble, tiredness of the spirit because they always forgot, always let themselves slide back into the old way of thinking and acting. And yet he loved them and they him. Flash was kneeling in front of him, had caught hold of his knees, was crying. Over their heads he saw his brother Simon, uncertain as always, yet—"James is not with you?"

"James said we were wrong—we must not interfere— with the powers of this world. . . ."

"Tell James," his elder brother said, "that I shall meet him again in three days' time." Then he said to the others: "I am going to the Temple."

"To the Temple—no!" said Rocky. "They'll only get you again!"

"Will you bar my Father's house to me?" said Jesus terribly, and walked away from among them.

"I can't bear it!" said Rocky suddenly. "Come, we must follow him, even if we die for it!"

"He won't let us," young John said, in misery. If only he could have explained that this rescue hadn't been his idea! Now he had to bear the blame with the others, the stupid fishermen! "We did wrong. May it be forgiven to us. And wiped out." Flash was sitting on the edge of the pavement, his head on his knees, crying his heart out.

But Malachi bar Joses had a horrible greenish look. After a while he vomited and it was mostly blood. Suddenly

Rocky said: "It's not too late—let me run after him—bring him back, he'd come back for that—he'll heal you!"

"No," said Malachi slowly, between gasps, and his voice had gone queer too: "I wouldn't—take my life—from him—the dirty traitor. He—couldn't have been—our Leader—the one we want—for Israel." His eyes shut for a moment, then flickered open just once more: "Not that man—but Bar Rabban."

Ten

ONE by one they trailed back, in various kinds of
misery and shame and bewilderment. Mat and the
Twin and the other James turned their backs on it all
and walked clean out of the city, not speaking to one another,
not looking at one another even. Bar Tolmai went the other
way towards Bethany; he could at least tell them there what
had happened. How their Master had left them to go to his
death. . . . But the friends of Malachi bar Joses took his
body away with them and remembered his words, and none
of them spoke to any of the Galileans.

"I'll have to—tell Mother," said Simon.

Slower and slower he walked back to the small room,
dragging his feet, Rocky, Stormy and Flash following. But
she knew, the moment she saw him. "He didn't—say
anything about any of us?" she asked. Perhaps—oh perhaps
he had thought of his mother.

"Only about James," said Simon, "there was some kind
of message for James. I'll have to try and remember."

Salome began in the background to wail and rock herself
about. It was all over now with Mary's son. But her own were
safe. She tried to get them to eat. It was not their fault that
the thing had been a failure.

After a while Mary said: "Did any of you get hurt?"

"None of us. Just that chap Malachi bar Joses. He got a
spear through that coat of his into his insides: a bit of bad
luck, right enough. He's dead."

Dead. The young Mary heard. Dead. With an immense
relief she accepted it, she slipped back into herself. But as

she did so she found, waiting inside her own mind, Malachi bar Joses with his lips out for her, but dead and killed in hard squares and triangles of blood and horror, purple and red and black, and, as she threw herself back away from it, she could not stop herself from screaming.

.   .   .   .   .

In the Temple Jesus of Nazareth waited. He did not preach. He did not so much as regard the stalls of the money-changers and the sellers of doves. All that was past. He went up a step and through the columns from the Court of the Gentiles to the inner court, the Court of the Women, and again through and up to the Court of Israel, knowing for sure that, in spite of blood and dirt and the defiling of the body, he was clean. Above and inward the smoke went up continually from the immense altar, the smoke of the old Law and the old Promise: which was now in action being reshaped and restated. This was his Temple, his place from childhood.

Yet perhaps it would be easier for them to take him in the outer court. He turned back and down and stood among the crowd, coming to worship, some truly, others between two wickednesses of anger or usury or cruelty, yet some half knowing what he wholly knew. Israel, he thought, my people, and the crowd flowed round him and the voices were like birds, like waves. And above in the north-west corner and only just outside the square of the Temple, the Romans leant over the parapet of their tower, looking down and totting up the value of old Herod's gold plates and bosses on the walls and doors.

Quite soon he was recognised. There was whispering, and then someone ran to tell Caiaphas, and Caiaphas on his knees thanked the God of his fathers, who had given this sign and would yet, through the death of only one man, save Israel. But Joseph of Arimathæa had also been told, for John

Priest had gone straight to him. He could not go back to the Ophel with the others, and he might not follow to the Temple. Joseph also saw it as the hand of God. "This is the final proof that he is innocent of all wrong!" he said. "Even the Sadducees must see it."

So he went hurrying off and met Caiaphas with some of the guards, on his way across to the Temple. It was two hours yet to noon, but it was going to be a blazing spring day. In the cracks of the stone walls there were green leaves and small white and yellow flowers.

"You have heard, then," said Joseph. "Is this something that a guilty man would do?"

"Certainly not," said Caiaphas, "nor is it something which would be done by a man who wanted to escape. I am not hurrying."

"So . . ." said Joseph, and they looked at one another while the guard waited. "You too believe him innocent?"

"I believe he must die," said Caiaphas.

"But surely, surely," Joseph said, "you dare not have the blood of an innocent man on your head? From the very beginnings the Lord our God has led us towards mercy! I would give mercy as I hope to have it myself. Yes, if I saw the least signs of innocence, even in a thief or a Sabbath-breaker."

"You Pharisees are not the only ones to value mercy, Joseph bar Achim," said Caiaphas, "though you seem to imply that you are. Nor would all your party agree with you. I can be merciful. . . . But this is not a case for—mercy." He stared at Joseph and shook his head: "I shall never be able to make you understand," he said, and called the guards to come on with him.

They came to the Temple, rich and heavy with history, and through to the outer court. Caiaphas went ahead. In a moment he came back and held up his hand to the guards. "Wait. He is praying. He will not try to escape." They

waited, not thinking of anything much. There were always a
lot of flies around here, because of the sacrifices. Every now
and then one of the guards would brush a fly off his face.

.   .   .   .   .

The legionaries, meanwhile, had reported the loss of their
prisoner, in face of overwhelming odds from the Jerusalem
mob. Everyone on their own side had behaved with
conspicuous gallantry. Roman casualties were restricted to
cuts and bruises, but some of the rebels had certainly been
accounted for. The centurion had a feeling that the whole
thing was rather unimportant; however, he in turn reported
it to Gaius Valerius Crispus. "I should think H.E. would be
quite relieved," said the paunchy young man. "Though I
hope it doesn't mean that the city mob is getting above
itself. It's this feast of theirs. There's always likely to be a
disturbance when they have a feast. Makes them think they're
something, I suppose."

"A feast," said the centurion. "Now, a feast ought to be
solemn. A procession of officials to a temple. A priestess with
garlands. The sacrifice competently done. Then everyone
goes home. That's my idea of what a feast ought to be like."

"It's not that way in the East," Gaius Valerius said. "But
you know that better than I do! And we must be tolerant.
Tolerant and as far as possible just. Trying to see the point
of view of the natives in so far as it is compatible with our
own authority."

"That's not so easy in practice," said the centurion.

"Far from it," said the young man, "especially in Judæa!"
He looked down towards the gate. There was a bustle going
on there, crossing and lowering of spears. "And here," he
said, "if I am not mistaken, comes our old friend, the
missing prisoner."

The centurion came and looked too: "Yes, by Jove, so it
is! I wonder what the devil has happened? I'd better go and
find out." In a few minutes he came back: "Yes, it is the

same one, Jesus the Galilean. It's the most extraordinary story. Herod found him not guilty, after messing about with him, I gather, but we all know what Herod can be like. Then, as we know, the mob rescued him and disappeared with him. Next thing he turns up in the Temple, waiting to be arrested again. Nobody with him. Nothing. Doesn't speak, of course. . . . And here he is."

"Most peculiar," said Gaius Valerius, "and I'm afraid His Excellency will be disappointed. He really thought he'd got rid of him nicely. I wonder what the explanation is? He struck me as being some kind of mystic."

"Dedicated to a god, perhaps," the centurion said.

"Funny if that's it," said Gaius Valerius, "and all these priests against him."

"Perhaps it's some other god."

"No, that can't be right; they've only got one here."

"Go on! That's only what they say. I've been about a bit, and there are always plenty of gods, whatever the natives tell you at first."

"You don't see temples to any other gods anywhere in Judæa."

"That's because you haven't looked long enough. Any city always has its biggest temple to its own special god who protects it officially. Athens, Ephesus. Ourselves for that matter. But there are always the others. And they may be a lot more powerful, you mark my words."

"This poor chap doesn't seem to have a very powerful god."

"Unless he's decided, in some way, to be a sacrifice. That kind of thing can happen."

"Well, I'm afraid H.E. won't be pleased to see him here again. Nor yet to see Caiaphas and his friends. You know, I don't like them myself. We've built them up, against their own mob, given them citizenship. That seemed to work in Gaul. Why, some of them behaved quite like ourselves, had the same way of looking at things. They wanted to be part

of the Empire. But these Jews, Cnæus, they never wanted
that. Funny, when you think of this wretched little country
of theirs. But they seem to imagine there's something special
about it. And the ones we've treated best, well, you feel
they'd knife you in the back as soon as look at you.
Patriotism and all that. But I sometimes wonder if we were
right to let them keep this Temple of theirs all to themselves,
not letting anyone but Jews near the altar. That's not
civilised. Imagine if we did it in Rome with one of the great
temples! No, that can't be allowed to go on indefinitely.
I know His Excellency feels the same. But whether he's been
quite wise over some of his methods . . ." The young
man looked worried; he knew rather too much. "And
this is the most awkward time for them to turn up, most
awkward. H.E. will be just about starting his lunch, and
he hates being interrupted. Oh well, he's sure to want me
as soon as he hears."

Eleven

WITH some apprehension Hector saw that this morning's prisoner was back, bringing with him, doubtless, all the morning's worries and agitations. Which meant—didn't it?—that the Tetrarch had come to no conclusion. Hector had hoped to have the afternoon off, perhaps at the cock-fight. Didn't look like it now. He grabbed at one of the slaves and told him to get over to the Residence and look sharp about it. He was to be sure to get word to Her Ladyship about this prisoner. "Why?" "Do as you're told!" But all the same, he'd like to know himself. According to Barsiné, Madame Joanna and Lady Claudia had talked for a long time about just this man. What was there about him, Hector thought, to get them all excited? He didn't see it. The man was just a country fanatic; he couldn't argue. As for his claims and his teaching, there had been, so he understood, two or three others who had put forward much the same type of claim to a special position or knowledge. If this man was a mystic, he seemed unable or unwilling to put it into words. After all, he couldn't even speak Greek. And there is only one language.

Claudia was reading; one of her friends in Rome had sent her some poems. Poetry was either indecent or dull. This was both. When Barsiné came with the message, she was quite glad of an excuse to roll up the book. She knew by now that this new prophet had been there in the morning and her husband had not found him guilty. It was a relief. She had not wanted to speak to him about the man.

Indeed she was never very anxious to speak to him about

88

anything serious. Their views did not coincide. It had, of
course, been a made marriage, though some people felt she
had been married beneath her. In a way, and especially at
the beginning when they were both quite young, they had
got on reasonably well. There was a son who had just
started on his army career; the daughter was with her aunt
in Rome who had her marriage arrangements in hand.
Another had died young. What did it all amount to? He had
his amusements; there was no open scandal. Much that he
did was admirable and she took pains to admire it when
possible.

But there was not much society in the province; Jerusalem
was, if anything, worse than Cæsarea. Gaius Valerius Crispus
was married, but his wife was rather a little ninny. There
were a few others, but the small group of Roman women
had said everything they ever had to say to one another; one
couldn't indefinitely rehash ancient gossip. Well, here was
something to be interested in. But perhaps dangerous. She
wondered how her husband would react to any message she
might send. She dropped her head on her hand, thinking it
over; Barsiné watched her anxiously, more and more
worried in case her mistress had been bewitched by this
magician.

.   .   .   .   .

The Procurator had been extremely annoyed when he
heard that his awkward prisoner had been brought back.
This time there were even more of the Jews in the outer
court of the Antonia, not only the respectable prosecutors
but a number of men who looked far from respectable,
among them, so Gaius Valerius whispered after listening to
a message which had come through to him, some of the
leaders of the mob. Apparently Caiaphas had specially asked
for them to be let in through the guarded gates of the
fortress. What kind of game was he playing now?

The accusations began again, and again the prisoner said

7—BYK

nothing. The Procurator signed to Hector to repeat everything that had been said in Greek in Aramaic. He was going to give the prisoner every chance. And, although Caiaphas and some of the others were speaking in Greek, there was plenty being yelled aloud which the prisoner might have answered—ought to have answered, blast him! thought Pontius Pilate. If he still doesn't answer we'll have to go through with the usual procedure. "Don't you hear what the witnesses are saying?" he asked. But it was no good.

There were more people in the great court now. It was difficult to tell just what they were all after. Surely some of them were bound to want the release of this prisoner, if, as the accusers said, he had such a following among the pilgrims? All right, he'd try it on. He stood up and said: "You will all remember that it is usual to amnesty one prisoner at the Passover. In this way you are reminded that the Divine Emperor is aware of his subjects and tempers justice with mercy. I propose to release this man whom you call the Christos."

This was translated and repeated. He expected at least some cheers, enough to justify him in the course he was proposing to take. But there was hardly any applause, instead shouts of "No! No! Not this one! Give us Bar Rabban!" "Who the devil is Bar Rabban?" said Pilate to Gaius Valerius, who reminded him that he was one of the ringleaders of the Tower of Siloam episode. "Have we got him?" Pilate asked.

"He's almost certainly in one of the lower prisons," said Gaius. "Shall I send and find out?"

"I'm damned if I shall give in to them," said Pilate, and his face flushed and neck thickened. This was some kind of put-up job. He remembered that the Tower riots were all in connection with the Corban money and his aqueducts. He wasn't going to let them get at him over that! If he released Bar Rabban or any of the others, it was a tacit admission that he had been wrong. No. He glanced at the prisoner. "Giving me no help," he said, "nor himself."

"If we adopted the usual procedure he might at least speak," Gaius Valerius said.

"All right," said the Procurator, "go ahead with it, but don't let them kill him. He doesn't look as if he could stand much."

Gaius sent down a message to the soldiers. They were to adopt the normal methods for a witness who was not a citizen and who proved difficult. In fact, slave's evidence was never taken without some kind of torture, but a free provincial, even though he was only a peasant, would be given a chance. This one had not taken the chance, so he would have to be whipped. It would not, however, be as severe a whipping as would have been ordered for a slave who had stolen something belonging to his master. It would draw blood, certainly, but not tear away lumps of muscle and skin.

While that was being done, the Procurator deliberately turned his back on the paved court and went into the judgment hall. It served them right for being a lot of hypocritical ritualists that they had to stay out there in the blazing sun, High Priest and all! He himself had a drink. "I hope they won't be able to make trouble for you, sir," said Gaius a little anxiously; "they've probably got plenty of friends in Rome."

"Now, what exactly do you mean by that?" Pilate asked.

This was an embarrassing question, since Gaius was not quite sure how much the Procurator thought he knew about certain things which had been going on. Methods of administration, naturally, varied from province to province; Pontius Pilate had not always been very subtle. Tribute has to be collected and of course a governor, of whatever rank, must be able to keep up appearances. There had been a few incidents. Gaius had felt that, occasionally, a little more patience and tact might have been used, especially considering that these natives of Judæa were notoriously awkward to handle and had in consequence been given various privileges from the central administration, in order, if possible, to attach them to Rome.

"The kind of thing I had in mind, sir," said Gaius cautiously, "would be if some of them were to hint that any aspect of your policy might have the result of alienating just those elements which have, so to speak, been cultivated. Not," he added hastily, for after all his own promotion depended mainly on the Procurator, "that you would not have ample justification for any action you may have taken."

"Bloody natives," said the Procurator, scratching under his official toga, "can't stand up to a beating." He was obviously thinking of some past incident, not of his present prisoner, who was, after all, only being induced to talk.

"The Divine Emperor," said Gaius, "has been known to act hastily. And on incorrect advice."

"We've left them far too much money, these priests," said Pontius Pilate, "but it's not so easy to get it off them."

"And they might use it—in Rome."

"As you say," said the Procurator. "Well, they should be through with this chap. Wonder if he'll talk? All nonsense of course; he hasn't done a thing. But he won't help himself."

One of the servants beckoned Hector to come over, and whispered to him. "Excuse me, sir," he said to the Procurator, "but there is a message from Lady Claudia—no, it is about this trial. She warns you, sir, to have nothing to do with the prisoner. It may be dangerous for you, sir, as she has reason to think he has certain powers. These, she says, were projected into a dream she had. She believes they are powers for good, and that the man is innocent."

"For once," said the Procurator, "I think my wife has said something sensible. But what the devil am I to do?"

The sergeant-in-charge had the prisoner untied. The man who had been on duty chucked the whip into a corner. There was a slight sprinkle of blood on the floor; it would wash off. "Get him into his coat again," the sergeant said. The prisoner had not cried out, only made little sounds and shivered; he wasn't as used to a beating as some they'd dealt with, and they hadn't laid it on too hard. They understood he was a teacher, anyhow someone fairly respectable. "Here, mate," he said, and helped him, not unkindly, into the wide sleeves of the linen coat. "Now, have a bit of sense and answer His Excellency's questions, so that it won't happen again."

They brought him through and the Procurator looked at him with great curiosity and the least touch of fear. Suppose his wife had really got something and the man had some kind of supernatural power? He might be sticking his head into something rather more dangerous than anything Caiaphas or his friends might be threatening. "Try to find out where he comes from, Hector," he said. "All this yarn about his being a Galilean peasant—it may be just their story. See if he won't tell you something about himself."

Hector went over to the prisoner and tried to be persuasive. If some of the stories were true, the man was a genuine wonder-worker, as Esdras seemed to think. It might be worth the Procurator's while to protect him, even to send him to Rome. The Emperor might be interested. But what was the use? Even after his beating the prisoner wouldn't say a word.

"All right," said Pilate, "tell him I can have him crucified; and will, if he doesn't talk. Rub it in, see? And tell him I can have him released. He mayn't understand that."

Hector repeated it. The prisoner looked up with those great eyes of his and spoke in a half whisper; nobody had given him anything to eat or drink since the evening before; why should they? It was none of their business. Hector translated: "He says, sir, that you would have no powers over him if you had not been given them from above. It was the ones who brought him to you who have done wrong."

"He seems to have a pretty good idea of the Imperial power!" said Pilate, half laughing. You might have expected the man to start asking for mercy; instead he'd reminded the Procurator that he was doing Cæsar's justice and had put the blame on the priests. Good for him! And the Procurator walked out into the paved court.

The yelling started again; it wasn't going to be easy. "The case against this man has not been made," the Procurator said in a loud voice. "I am releasing him."

But there seemed to be more than ever in the crowd, not only the priests but a lot more, madly excited, rushing up against the guards and getting knocked in the face and yelling for the release of this Bar Rabban. They'd got it into their heads that he was going to be let out—or might be if they yelled enough. And apparently the priests were encouraging them. "The man has been beaten for creating a disturbance," said the Procurator, hoping that this might quiet them, "and I am now freeing him." But some of them were beginning to yell at him to crucify the prisoner. A bloodthirsty lot; why couldn't they have killed the man themselves if they'd wanted to? He listened for a moment. Yes, there it was, the yelling voices gathering rhythm, becoming percussive; they had a slogan now—or someone had given it to them: "We want Bar Rabban!" It had become a kind of delightful chant. Intolerable! For a moment the Procurator considered the possibility of getting rid of them; giving the order to the legionaries who were being marvellously patient so far, had hardly drawn blood. Now—if they charged these hell-cats of Jews, it would be something they'd deserved for months, and he might get rid of some of the worst. No, better not. It would get reported in Rome. Exaggerated. His poor lads must put up with it a bit longer. Gods, what a province!

The centurion in command of the guard came up, saluted and handed him a small roll of parchment. He straightened it out and looked at it, frowning; when he

looked up he saw Caiaphas watching him, and after a
moment gestured to him to come nearer. "Yours, I take it?"
he said, furious and rather alarmed.

"A reminder," Caiaphas said: "some of us merely wished
to point out that this man is considered as a king by—a great
many of our people, unfortunately. The ignorant and
rebellious, of course. But the rest of us feel very strongly that
this is a capital offence and that the release of the man must
be considered as a definitely—unfriendly act towards
Tiberius Cæsar. It would be reported as such. We understand
that Cæsar is—sensitive. And I would remind Your
Excellency that a number of us, including myself, are Roman
citizens owing loyalty to the Emperor." He bowed and
withdrew to the front of the crowd. Nobody else had heard
exactly what he said, but most had guessed.

"I'll get him for that—one day," said Pilate half aloud.
Well, he'd try just one more thing. This damned crowd,
surely if what the priests had said was half true there'd have
been a few who wanted the man released! Enough to give
him an excuse. Or had the accusers managed to pack the
place with the Bar Rabban crowd? It looked like it, but still,
if they saw the poor chap—they were always supposed to be
a merciful lot.

He said a word to Hector, who hurried back into the
judgment hall and told them His Excellency wanted the
prisoner shown to the crowd. The soldiers brought him out
and one of them pulled back the coat to show the bloodstains
and bruises where he had been well and truly punished for
making a disturbance. "You see," said the Procurator, "this
is the one who was called your king." His own voice had
considerable pity in it, and Hector, translating, added, for
the sake of the crowd, that this miserable piece of beaten
flesh was all that was left of the king, they might as well let
it go.

Yes, it did seem that there were other voices—even a few
priests who had made their way in—"From the other

party," whispered Gaius. And quite a few shouts, but the crowd was fighting among itself, and it looked as if the Bar Rabban lot had got the upper hand. The chant went on louder, with clapping and stamping of feet. It would be stones next. And half of them joining in just for the hell of it, no doubt! No use risking Roman lives to stop that. "Crucify him!" they yelled. And suddenly the Procurator found himself utterly sick of them. "You really wish me to have this poor chap crucified?" he said.

Caiaphas answered: "It is Cæsar who would wish it."

"Very well, then," said the Procurator, "the cross it is." He spoke to the sergeant: "Take him through to them and say my orders are that he is to be crucified. And they'd better look sharp about it." He didn't look at the prisoner again. What was the use? He'd done his best. The accusers appeared to want to thank him; he turned his back on them. Gaius reminded him of something. "Oh yes, get hold of Bar Rabban. See that he's cleaned up a bit before you release him. I hope they'll be pleased, blast them."

"Did you want something put on to the cross, sir?" Gaius asked.

"Yes," said the Procurator, "that's an idea. I'll think about that one. Gaius, do you suppose this chap was—the kind of thing my wife seems to have thought? Did he have some kind of—powers?"

"It's possible, sir," Gaius said, "were you thinking—of some kind—of protective ceremony?"

"Best to be on the safe side," said the Procurator, "I don't want trouble with spirits. Or any kind of foreign gods or powers. Bring me a basin and some water. We'll just go into the inner room."

It was a relief to be there with his own protecting gods, brought with such care from the old home, the Lares of the house. Even the thought of them cut him off from the yelling of the crowd and the threats of the Sadducee party. So old, so benign. He murmured a few words and made the traditional gestures, as his fathers had done before him through all the years of the greatness and security of Rome. Gaius brought the water and poured it over his hands, absolving him, through the power of the element, from blood guilt, making a barrier between him and any supernatural anger, deflecting it from him and his household, especially his wife. Together they spoke the age-old sentences of protection, the ancient questions and answers. As he came out, Pilate thought he would tell his wife that this had been done; he felt a sudden curious affection for her, another Roman in a strange and rather nasty land.

Twelve

WHEN they came for him, struck the pins out of the shackles, and shoved him through the door, Bar Rabban had no idea what was to happen. He thought that probably they were taking him to execution, and began to repeat to himself the prayers for one about to die: May my death be an atonement for all sins. . . . Nobody said anything, but prodded him up the stone stairs; he stumbled, not having been able to walk more than three or four steps in either direction for long months. Was it going to be the cross or the sword, or perhaps burning alive? A man's courage goes out of him after a long time in the dark, on bread and water. He thought hard about the Maccabees and other heroes of his people, farther back, who had suffered bravely and said scornful words at the end, taunting their enemies. If only he could do that! Difficult to think of anything to say, now. If it had been earlier, in hot blood after the fighting at the Tower! Now, by his reckoning, it should be almost the time of Passover. To have to die just before that. Hard on a man. Round a corner they came into light, and he threw his hand up over his eyes. Odd to be able to move one's arms freely again. He would rather die in daylight, but this violent sun—and it wasn't even sun, just an ordinary room, a guardroom full of uninterested soldiers. There was a brown water-pot, a towel and a comb. "Go on, wash!" said someone. He supposed he was to be taken before some tribunal to be formally condemned, and washed slowly, every now and then shutting his eyes and then opening them again. Someone came up behind and cut his hair to shoulder level. Another one threw over a clean tunic. His old rags tore off him at a pull.

Where now? He was marched through a passage, across some kind of storeroom full of army equipment, along another passage at right angles. They came to a heavy door, with bolts that had to be tugged back. Beyond that, perhaps, was his death. Lord God of Israel, have mercy on your poor soldier. . . . He walked through steadily and stood on a step. Below, people. As he began to take them in, the soldier beside him shouted, "Here is that prisoner you asked for," and stepped back, shutting the door with a great slam. And then the voices, the arms stretched out, the cries: "Bar Rabban, Bar Rabban! You have come back to us! Back to us alive, our leader, Jesus bar Rabban!" And at last he understood.

.   .   .   .   .

The centurion was watching, leaning over the top of the wall. Pity this had been done. But H.E. must have had his reasons. He supposed it would be guard duty over the crosses. Not the pleasantest part of a soldier's routine, but had to be done. And why was the High Priest coming back in such a hurry?

"He wants to see me again? I dare say," said the Procurator, "but I've had my lunch interrupted once already."

"Hadn't you better, sir?" Gaius said anxiously.

"I know what it's about, of course. Oh well, perhaps you're right." The Procurator got up and strolled into the paved court. It was almost noon and he could feel the heat on the stones coming up through his sandals. Caiaphas had a wooden board in his hand, which the Procurator recognised. Hector had written it out in the three official languages to an exact wording: *Jesus of Nazareth, the King of the Jews.*

Caiaphas was shaking with anger. "Your Excellency has

been pleased to make a joke in poor taste," he said. "It will be taken very badly. Very badly indeed."

"Indeed?" said Pontius Pilate. "I should have thought you would have approved. Shows what happens to people who make themselves out to be kings in a Roman province."

"But that's it!" said Caiaphas, "you've only to alter it so as to read, 'He said "I am king of the Jews".' Doesn't Your Excellency see that this other way is—an insult?"

"An insult?" said Pilate. "Who to? You?"

"Yes."

"Ah," said Pilate. "Well, it's written now—see? Go and put it back." He looked at the High Priest, smiling more and more broadly, then went back to his lunch with an admirable appetite.

.   .   .   .   .

Down in the courtyard of the Antonia the men were putting in time on one of their favourite knuckle-bone and dice games. The marks were scratched on the flagstones, so that you didn't even have to chalk them in, the letters and squares, the sword, the crown, the scorpion, and so on. If you got the King throw it was just too bad; the rest had the right to make a show of you. For that matter, the game went away back to the old, old days and something that wasn't rightly a game at all. In those days the King was the sacrifice in real earnest, not just the one that had a bucket of water thrown at him.

So now one of the soldiers had just had the dirty throw and the rest were prepared to get a hold of him, when a condemned Jew was shoved in, of all people the one who'd said he was King. What a piece of luck! They all made a dash at him and hoisted him up on the steps just near where the game was. He couldn't understand what was going on, poor chap; looked all to bits anyway. But they wrapped a bit of an old purple rug round him. His hands were tied so they stuck a reed into them for a sceptre. "Give him a crown!"

said someone, and another one twisted up a crown out of the thorny bits of kindling by the cookhouse door. "Fine!" they said, "that's right! Hail, King!" and burst into shouts of laughter. And the poor King stood on the steps, without a notion of what was going on, and after a while the crucifixion party, with a centurion in charge, came to take him off.

It was not very far to the place of execution. The three condemned men had to pick up their own cross-beams and carry them there. The other two had already been sentenced; it was a matter of convenience when the sentence was to be carried out. Robbery with violence was the crime. They stared at the third, wondering vaguely who he was. One of them refused to pick up the piece of heavy wood, till he got a good kick from one of the soldiers. He began to yell. "Keep that till you need it!" the soldier said and hit him over the mouth. It was intolerable if they started howling already. The third one seemed to be genuinely trying to pick up and carry the piece of wood he was going to be nailed on to, but just couldn't manage it. "Here," said the soldier, and gave it a heave up, but noticed that the man was still shaky and bleeding a bit after his whipping; probably that was what was the matter. There was a small crowd, looking on, staring as usual. The soldier caught hold of one of them, a stranger and solid looking, and ordered him to pick it up and carry it. The man protested violently, frightened and angry, and the rest of the crowd protested too, except those who thought it best to get away quickly. Just like the Romans, wasn't it, to make an innocent man carry a cross for some criminal! And it turned out that he was a respectable pilgrim from the Jewish community at Cyrene, who had come to Jerusalem for Passover; a terrible piece of luck for a man, to have to carry a cross! It was to be hoped it wouldn't follow him back to his home town. Oh, these Romans!

"Sarah! Rachel! Come now, oh come out, come out for the wailing!"

"Who are they crucifying now?"

"Three poor souls, all ready for their last walk. Two patriots that were caught at the good work and this one that looks near his end already. . . ."

"Ah, that's the one from Galilee, Mary of Nazareth's son that they tell these stories about. Some said he was going to be king. . . ."

"It's a high, high throne he's walking to now, and not a friend by him. . . ."

"Maybe they're all scared. Or maybe they don't know. But his poor mother should be by him now if word could be got to her. Ah, the wicked Romans, nailing our poor lads up on their great tyrannous crosses! But some day we shall be on top of them and there'll be glory for the unfortunate patriots! But we'll give them a good noble wailing on the walk they're set on and it'll take their minds off what's to come. . . ."

A good sound wailing by women who practise it often and are proud of their abilities will carry a long way. The houses echo it and it blows across from one quarter to another, a shrill, throbbing thread of sound, not to be ignored. Rocky dropped his head in his hands. "He didn't want us. He sent us away. Not to be there with him; that's our punishment."

Flash said: "I've been thinking. And it came to me. He's set to die all alone out there. And he's handed his life over to us, to live it if we can. He said there'd be terrible sorrow for us, but it would clear in the end and turn into joy."

" 'In a little while', he said, but how can we ever have anything but sorrow the rest of our lives?"

"I don't know, Rocky, I don't know. But I think we've got to live through this. Where's John Priest?"

Stormy shook his head. "He went off alone. Mother's getting ready to go."

"How's Miss Mary, Flash? Is she set on going?"

"Yes. In spite of everything. But she's got a terrible look on her, as if—as if——"

"Yes, I know. If she starts screaming again . . ."

The three women were all dressed alike in black cloaks that hid their dresses which showed by cut and embroidery patterns that they were Galileans; nor would you know that two were old and one young. They said very little, only the old Mary quivered and then caught herself up from time to time, like a tree in a terrible gust of wind. It still did not seem possible that this was certainly going to happen. Yet every time they heard the wailing it became surer. She had heard it before, thinking with pity about the poor criminals going to meet their due. Now, impossibly, it was her own son.

As they walked through the little narrow streets of the Ophel, up and round, they were everywhere going past other women scrubbing their tables and pots, getting ready for the Sabbath. There was a cheerful noise going past them all the time, neighbours calling to one another. For some it would be Passover as well, but for all it was the Sabbath coming towards them like a bridegroom. For other women, but not for them.

The condemned, too, could see the preparations going on, though any woman would hurriedly pick up her things and take them indoors, not to be touched by their shadow. Yet they saw it, one especially. If he could have been let alone, to enter into death step by step, fully certain of every separate one, fully accepting the experience. But the wailing bored into him, infinitely distressing, keeping him from the solitary, unsharable experience. He asked them not to weep and wail for him, but it went on. He shook his head. "Weep for yourselves and your children," he said, "for the bad days are coming." And then, in one of his old riddling sentences: "If they do these things in a green tree, what shall be done in a dry?"

What is the man talking about? Trees? A dry tree, the centurion thought to himself, and was suddenly reminded of the sacrificial tree of the great Baal of Syria, decked and decorated with sacrifices. He gave orders to keep the crowd

a bit farther away. Not that there would be any attempt at a
rescue, but all this howling and muttering got on his nerves.
They went out of the city by the Gennath gate; a moment of
shadow cut out from the blazing sun. In a few minutes they
had passed an enclosure of high hurdles, for goats perhaps,
and a few rickety sheds that hid from sight what suddenly
shouted at them: the black uprights of the crosses stuck and
waiting for them in the dry hill.

That always checked the condemned a step or two and
sent the wailing up a jump. The guard knew it well, were
ready to give the blow which would jolt the criminals into
the next step. But it was curious that the third man, the one
who had seemed so exhausted, was now the only one to
continue walking as though this were some ordinary goal.
Perhaps he was a little mad.

They turned right and halted among the rocks in the
waste ground. There were a dozen or so of these black
uprights. Sometimes they were all full. The sight of them was
salutary, reminding potential bandits, murderers and rebels
of what had happened to others and what waited for them.
The centurion pointed out three. Then he posted his guard.
Their immediate job was to keep the crowd off; there was
always the possibility of a nasty rush. You could see where
people were coming hurrying out of the gate after them so
as not to miss the fun. There would be bound to be some
women too; sometimes they'd try everything to get the
guards to let them come a bit nearer. He wondered if there
would be any special trouble about this man who was
supposed to have set himself up as a king. Probably not,
probably his subjects had crawled back into the gutter too
scared to move. Anyway, it was only the pilgrims from the
country, not the real tough mob. Had it been a sensible
move, letting them have that Bar Rabban back? Well,
anyway, most of them would be so pleased about that they
wouldn't care what was happening to this other one. The
man from Cyrene who had been pressed into carrying the

cross-beam had put it down gingerly, taken one look at the
guards, and then, seeing they were done with him, had
begun to creep away. One of them, for a lark, had shouted
after him and he'd run like a rat.

The actual nailing wasn't the soldiers' job. They supervised
the natives who always did it. But they did have certain
perquisites. One of them had his eye on the coat this king
fellow was wearing: a nice bit of stuff, good linen, probably
given him by some woman. He knew just the place to sell it.
That didn't go down with the rest, though, so they decided
to throw sixes for it as soon as the main job was done. It
would pass the time. There was nothing on the other two
worth having.

The centurion stood in front, watching the crowd for
trouble, his back to what was going on up the hill. It was
always a bit unpleasant unless one of the criminals was
someone particularly vicious; if so, of course, it was a
pleasure. One or two of his men always got a kick out of it,
though; it made a change. There was the usual screaming
and cursing and the whack of the nails being driven in, the
screams changing tone, becoming suddenly desperate and
then dropping into sobbing. When there were only three it
didn't take that long. What would it be like, the centurion
wondered, for someone who really thought he was a king?
But perhaps he hadn't. His Excellency seemed to think it
was all nonsense. Probably he'd made enemies and they'd
managed to get back on him. That happened. It didn't
concern the occupying forces, anyway. Or, if he was a
magician, maybe he didn't feel pain. That was an idea. The
centurion turned to look. Yes, they'd got him on to the
cross-beam all ready to haul up. His eyes were shut and
lower lip caught under teeth; his thin chest heaved
spasmodically. No, he didn't seem to be a magician. At any
rate he appeared to be feeling as much pain as anyone else.
Naturally, it was a painful way of dying; society cannot
exist without efficient deterrents. Civilised society, that is.

ı—BYK

The centurion gave the word to haul up and the screaming started again as the strain came on the nailed hands and the flesh tore. The bodies heaved and collapsed with pain. The fingers on the hands, and the toes on the nailed feet, writhed. "Get the labels up!" said the centurion. "No, idiot—it's the man in the middle that's the king. Get it firm."

The crowds could now be allowed nearer; the time for attempted rescue was over and the deterrent effect at its height. A few respectable people would be allowed the first look. Yes, here was a little party of them, clean robes, good shoes, shaved faces, who quite ignored the wretched bandits in order to stare at the middle one. That board over his head seemed to annoy them. They read it, whispered to one another, pointed. Another two or three came and joined them and began jeering at the man on the cross, whose eyes fluttered momentarily open to look at them. One of them threw a clod of earth and prickles, but the guard stopped that; people couldn't be allowed to do just what they liked. This was an official execution.

Thirteen

THERE was a guild of charitable ladies who paid for a kind of drug based on myrrh, which could be given to those publicly tortured, as by crucifixion. It did not immediately lessen the pain, but blurred the mind so that the pain stood away a little. The authorities condoned it.

From the edge of the crowd the three women watched and saw one of the bandits eagerly sucking it off the sponge which the guild's man held out to him on the end of a stick. He had been screaming on and off, but now that died down into a kind of witless chant. The man went on to the middle cross, dipped the sponge into the jar and reached up. The old Mary was whispering to herself, "Take it, my darling, take it!", as though the one on the cross were a sick child refusing a cup of milk. But he shook his head and shut his lips. "Why not?" said the old Mary. "Oh, why not?"

It was the young Mary who answered, timidly and yet with certainty: "Because he has to face—everything—with his mind clear. Isn't it that?"

"Yes," said the old one. "Yes, child. But if only I could bear part of it for him! If only. You know, when he was a little boy . . ." But she couldn't go on. The one on the farther cross had taken his myrrh now.

"He hasn't seen us, not yet, the poor boy," said Salome; "he didn't want to look when those others were going for him, and he hasn't opened his eyes again."

"He used to go that way, shut inside himself," the mother said, "as though he were listening, as though he was open to —something else. Not just us. I used to get angry with him,

try and get him to attend. Especially before strangers, when
I wanted them to—to see who he was. And perhaps I didn't
know myself." She dabbed at her eyes with the edge of her
veil. "If only I could get nearer, so he could see—we hadn't
deserted him."

The young Mary went up to the nearest guard and spoke
in hesitant Greek, for she knew a little: "Can you let us
come nearer? It is—the mother—and mother's sister."

"Against orders to let you pass, miss," said the man, "but
I can stand a bit farther back—see? That is, if you keep
quiet. Can't have any disturbance, you know." And he
walked in a brisk and official manner a certain distance away.

"Come," said young Mary and took the two older ones by
the hand. They hung back a little, scared of the soldiers; you
never knew what a soldier might do; you expected something
bad. Salome was thinking all the time that it might have
been one of her own boys. Might be yet, if they were caught.
So long as they stayed away now! Mary's poor boy up there,
with the flies beginning to come after the blood. On his
hands they were now, and round his mouth and eyes. And he
couldn't so much as brush them off.

Now there was another crowd who pushed past the
women, shoving aside the old Mary so that she tumbled to
her knees. The soldier, however, stopped them from getting
any nearer. "That's the one I heard preaching!" a man
shouted. He was wearing a long coat with a silk stripe
woven in it and fur round the neck; a successful merchant
perhaps. "In the Temple itself—shouldn't have been
allowed! Saying he could tear it all down, our new Temple,
the wonder of the world!"

Another of them looked at the crosses with a curling lip:
"He said he was the son of God—that—that *thing* up there!
Disgusting."

"Son of God indeed! The filthy blasphemer. Mark my
words, there's punishment coming for having let him live so
long! As if *he* could be the Chosen One!" Suddenly it was all

too much and the man yelled up: "Son of God, you! Come down off that cross and show us!"

"Ah," said another, an older man, "he's got what he was due. But do you see what the Romans have gone and put up over him? Shameful, that is; couldn't someone have stopped them?"

"They say the High Priest, the Lord be with him, tried, but this Procurator of ours treated him like dirt—like dirt! All that one's fault—ah, you! Wish I could get at you!" He shook his fist and spat. The guard picked his teeth; he understood a word here and there. Excitable types, these.

.   .   .   .   .

"You aren't hurt, Mother?" Someone was helping Mary to her feet. She whispered, more to herself than him: "I wish I were." Then she turned: "But—is it safe for you to be here?"

"I think so," said John Priest; "besides—I'm not sure I care much."

"Did you still hope—it wouldn't happen?" the young Mary asked. She was standing very still and shivering.

"I suppose so," said John Priest. "There are some things one can't believe until the moment comes. He knew what he was risking when he came to preach the new way in Jerusalem. He knew how so many of our people were bound to feel—the ones who can bear anything, but not a change. He knew the black pit of hate he was walking into. But can he have known it was sure? Whatever part Judas had in it, the trap would have snapped. And the ones who thought he was just a king coming to take possession of a kingdom were no help!" He looked rather bitterly at Salome, stupid Salome who really had thought her two sons were going to be princes and generals!

"What is he thinking now?" the young Mary asked. "I can't—oh, I can't look." She had a feeling as though, if she looked, something would burst inside her. And that mustn't happen—not yet; she was here to be with his mother. And get her home afterwards.

John looked and looked away, and looked again, burning his eyes. "Is he thinking? Is it possible to think? He is in very great pain. Perhaps he is only suffering. Perhaps he is counting the time. It will seem to him to have stopped. But he has only been there a very short while; by our time. Hours to go before it is over. Hours. And then, rest. By tonight he will be with his Father." He said nothing for a moment, then suddenly with horrible impatience: "I wish I could kill those flies!"

.   .   .   .   .

It was a boring job, guard duty at a crucifixion. Nothing going on. Even an impalement was more interesting, for at least the man could wriggle. The centurion had never seen a mass crucifixion as they had sometimes for rebels, or slaves who had revolted. Some of them might last up to three days, the real tough ones. One of the bandits looked a bit droopy. "Tickle him up, there!" the centurion said. One of the soldiers jabbed him with a spear. Oh yes, he was alive all right; gave a real good jerk, tore at his hands, yelped. "I remember one crucifixion," one of the soldiers said. "It was the second day, and some of them were dead. There were a lot of those pariah dogs about; nasty brutes, started licking at the blood. Well, we weren't bothering ourselves much till we heard an extra squawking, and do you know this, those dogs had started eating the feet off one of them. He wasn't dead at all!"

"It used to give me a bit of a thrill," one of the others said gloomily. "Now it doesn't. It would give me a thrill to nail up a woman. Yes, it would."

"Ah. That would be something. That would certainly be something," said his friend.

The centurion looked with some curiosity at the one in the middle, the one who had set himself up as king and talked about trees. Why hadn't he taken the dope? Mad not to take it when it was offered. They were a queer lot, those Jews. He'd had a Jewish slave once, a nice, bright boy; but obstinate. Wouldn't eat ordinary, decent food, sooner starve, wouldn't work on this day of theirs; not if you beat him black and blue. He'd had to give in to it in the end, let the boy go his own silly way. And he was grateful! Came and kissed his hand. A funny lot!

Having got a yelp out of one of the bandits, the soldiers tried the other, with an equally amusing effect. The man started cursing away at them; they laughed and laughed. Then they tried the middle one. They got a cry all right but it wasn't out of the man; it was out of the old woman crouching on the rock all out of shape like a bird brought down by a stone. The man himself opened his eyes and said very loud and just as if he was talking to someone: "Father, forgive them. They do not know what they are doing." One of the soldiers translated to the others. That was a queer thing to say and no mistake. "Well, I know what I'm doing," he said, "don't have to be told!" And he shortened his spear for another jab.

But the others stopped him; it mightn't be lucky. Made you feel something had gone wrong. One of them told the centurion. "Yes," he said, "better leave him alone, men. For the moment. He may be dedicated in some way. Besides, I didn't like the way that crowd of street pedlars over there" —and he pointed to the respectable group—"were getting a kick out of it. No, we're not here to please *them*." And he took another turn round the bit of rough land where the crosses were, just to see that there was no sign of a disturbance anywhere. In one place some of them were still chanting away at that stupid slogan of theirs, clapping their hands in time to it. "Stop that!" he said, and after a few ragged boos it stopped. Some of them even went off back to the city, looking half ashamed.

Fourteen

JAMES, who was also called Judge, or the Just, was on his way home to his own community, away over towards Jordan, once more turning his back on the world. As always the world had shown itself for what it was, suddenly averting its fair face and showing the rotten and stinking hollow of its back.

You left your own place where all was ordered and directed towards one end, the end of the Lord God, the God of Israel, the place where evil could be stripped off like dirty rags; whose waters cleansed off more than the dust of roads; where a man need no longer fret himself with choices, since there was only one choice. Thinking intently of this, he walked south out of the Ophel, up and down steps, past places where the naked rock showed between low houses, his back to the Temple, the gold and the ivory. He did not notice the people he was walking past, as his brother would have noticed, seeing those who were unhappy or ill and reaching out to them, so that, if they were to turn his way, he would be ready.

James did not see the children playing, nor the dark-eyed little girls with bunches of tulips and field flowers, scarlet and yellow, nor the women carrying jars or heavy baskets on their heads. And the women avoided him and his pure linen, aware that, however clean they might be, he would think their touch defiling. They turned their backs on him and his robe and his great stick; that kind of holiness! He just noticed the street of the frying, since smells get through a mind barrier more easily than sights. He remembered how as a child he had liked one special sort of fried cake, and his mother would sometimes get him one, though not so often as she would get special things for her first-born.

His mother. He had gone to Jerusalem to see her in her trouble and she had snatched at him—even in an old one, the terrible smell of women! He had gone, as she had asked him, to see what had happened to Jesus, the eldest. It was, perhaps, his duty to the family to do that. And it was as everyone might have known it would be. His brother Jesus had looked for God, not, as must be, by shutting out the world and destroying in his heart all the images of the world, but by trying to make the world and the men and women in the world one with God. Which is impossible.

So he was taken by the powers of the world. And would be destroyed by them. Yet perhaps that proved that he was a true teacher, since it had always happened. James thought of the past, the long history of the teachers, preachers and prophets of Israel: how could they not be against the dark powers? He thought of the Master of Righteousness two generations back and his new covenant; he thought of John the prophet who had dipped him in Jordan and cleansed him from the sins of being human. There were certain kinds of words which all of them had spoken, making a body of knowledge: the way of the Lord, things found in Mount Sinai by Moses first but now enlarged. Could there, he wondered, be prophets among the Gentiles? No, how could it be so when the Gentiles were all tangled up with their dark gods?

He sat down on a stone and began to think about his brother, turning over in his mind the things which his brother, too, had said. He had been there himself on many occasions and had sometimes been tempted to think that, after all, it was true and that his brother Jesus was Messiah. He had even thought so for a moment in the early morning, after hearing how things had gone in the house of Annas. But then, this rescue that they had all gone off on before he left. The Messiah would not need to be rescued by men, not by wild and reckless and sinful men like these fishermen; men who had gone with women, who had been drunk and fought and taken the Lord's name in vain. Even if you repent and turn from such ways you are soiled, you are no more gracious in the sight of God. His brother was for ever speaking of forgiveness. As though the cracked jar could ever carry water.

And yet, yet—if he were the One foretold. He had walked in the footsteps of those before him, who, also, had preached a new way and a new power, who had seen a brotherhood of the poor and the folly of possessions! He had gone into the wilderness and wrestled with the evil dream of power. It was while he was in the wilderness that James had first begun to think about this brother of his in a special way. But Jesus had come back into the world, wandering round with these wild friends of his and breaking the rules, becoming angry, crying over his dead friend Lazarus. And what had happened there? Perhaps Lazarus had not been truly dead. He knew his brother had powers of healing; there was that time when he, James, had been bitten by a viper. He was only a small child and he had caught hold of a bright slithery thing in the dust and it had turned. He remembered now how he had screamed and his mother had screamed and his arm began to swell, and then Jesus, who was working at the bench with his father, learning his trade, had come running and handled his arm, and the pain and the swelling slowly left it. But to raise the dead? If he had been able to do that he could not need to be rescued, carried off and hidden like a stolen penny. No, that could never happen to the Chosen of God.

There was a shout, from some way off. He knew the voice and looked round. It was his brother Simon, running, shouting for him. What had happened now? He waited and Simon caught up with him, panting. Simon was a little frightened of him. It was hard on a man to have two brothers he couldn't understand. "Well?" said James, "did you—succeed?"

Simon looked at the ground in front of his brother's feet. He started speaking and stopped. At last he said: "Our brother is being crucified—now."

James swallowed: "So—you did not succeed."

"We did," Simon said, "but he wouldn't let us get him away. He walked back: into their hands."

"I see," said James. Then with great intentness: "Was Lazarus of Bethany truly dead?"

"Lazarus? Oh yes," said Simon. "And then they took him again. In the Temple. And the Roman gave orders to crucify him."

"Did he—say anything—before he went back?"

"He was angry with us, said we didn't understand. And there was a message for you. I'd forgotten. He said—but it seems—oh James, you are so much wiser, what do you make of it? He said I was to tell you—he would meet you again in three days' time. James! Where are you going?"

"I am going to the place of crucifixion."

James turned and walked back the way he had come, back into the world, and Simon trotted after him, not daring to ask questions, but worrying about the others back in Nazareth. They wouldn't know for a day or two and they might take fright when they heard. And likely enough the neighbours might pick it up wrong and think it was a good excuse for breaking in and smashing up the business. That nice new delivery of cedar wood! If only he could trust Jude and Jose to have some sense, but they might get scared. It's not easy when your elder brother gets crucified for— whatever it was; the things he'd said might get twisted. One of the brothers-in-law was sure to make trouble. Oh it was going to be difficult for the family!

They crossed round the foot of the Ophel hill, almost through the dung heaps, but James didn't seem to notice. He was talking to himself, and every now and then he

repeated in a quite loud voice one of the things his brother
had said. Now the south wall of the Temple hung above them
in the high blue air with the sun striking against it and
glittering on stone and brass, and the throng of people on
the broad steps like bees alighting. But they turned west and
up. There were steps here in the rock, and James went up
them steadily and quickly like a strong mule. From there
under the archway and again up, and so through the main
city, the stone houses of the rich, the sounds of singing and
women from behind shutters, the shops of the goldsmiths
with their guards standing easy beside them but with clubs
in their hands, and everywhere the Passover crowds, about
their business or staring, even Gentiles among them, up from
the coast or in from farther east, for this would be a time for
useful contacts. But the thin ill-darned linen of the Essenes
was something which could always get by; Israel knew and
was a little proud, a little afraid, and partly seeing them as a
useful barrier between themselves and an immense, alarming
and incomprehensible God.

So the two brothers went through the city and out at the
gate. There on a little hillock with the great dry valley down
to the left were the crosses and their eldest brother stripped
and still on one of them. Simon choked and wiped his sleeve
across his eyes.

.   .   .   .   .

There was more of a crowd now, and two or three times it
seemed likely to flare up, all over this one in the middle. The
bandits may have had their wives and mothers watching
them, but, if they did, nobody bothered. But it was clear to
the centurion that there were quite a few who were bitterly
angry and grieved over this king of theirs. Country people,
they looked like, mostly, the kind that have a few olive trees
and a few sheep; free provincials. Why had the Procurator
gone and done this just before their big feast? Oh well,
political pressure, he supposed. . . . He would never

understand politics. Thank the gods, he was only a soldier!

He sent a squad here and there to break things up if any of the men looked like coming to blows with one another, for there definitely were two lots in this crowd. Naturally one had to use a certain respect in moving on those who might perhaps be Roman citizens. His men knew enough to recognise a priest. He didn't suppose that the High Priest would be there, but there might be some of his party, even his relations. He'd heard this man was an enemy of theirs, or anyway a danger to them.

One of his men pointed out a real sight: a frail-looking young chap leaning with one hand on a stick, the other on the shoulders of a woman: "That's the one that was raised from the dead, sir!"

"Now that's interesting," said the centurion; "what does he say it was like being dead?"

"Seems he can't remember, sir. Like being asleep."

"Well, he's missed an opportunity. Think of that—being dead and not remembering a thing about it!" The centurion looked up; it was getting dark; one of these storms blowing up.

.   .   .   .   .

It seemed to the old Mary that if she could stand on a certain rock and call to him, her son would open his eyes and know her. This rock was about a quarter of the way between her and the foot of the cross; there was a tuft of dusty wild hyssop growing by it with a few small yellow flowers still hanging on it. Yet it was a world away.

Suddenly the young Mary was pulling at her: "Come nearer! They are letting everyone move." And that was so. As those on the crosses weakened, it seemed harmless to allow the crowd a rather better view. The little group all went forward, timidly; they reached the rock and now Mary was near enough to be able to call to her son.

He opened his eyes and looked dizzily downward,

uncertain whether this voice out of the past, as all his life by now was past, was a real voice. The outward effort showed that it was all still going on. Even the slight, careful movement of his head sharpened the pain again. He tried to smile, but it seemed as though those muscles had ceased for ever. Yet he must change the look in her face. John too. They would go on living in the ordinary way, while he. . . . Don't let him look at me, said the young Mary to herself; not now, not now. If he looks at me something will break! He did not look at her, nor yet at old Salome. He gathered himself to build one more bit of the Kingdom, saying to his mother, "There is your son now", and to John, "There is your mother". Between them, some barrier would be broken, some new deeps would be reached. He shut his eyes again.

"Yes," said John, "Yes!" and caught old Mary in his arms. And as he did so he saw James and Simon, who were now his brothers, standing at one side. James was very still, watching, watching. But Simon had his hands up over his eyes; he could not find it in him to watch.

Fifteen

AS the effect of the myrrh drug wore off, the bandits woke to pain and flies and dragging time and the human need to blame someone else. One of them started off on this king—his fault, setting the Romans on them, letting on he was the Messiah! After a bit the other one shouted back at him to shut up, they were all going to meet their God together; the two of them had got what was coming to them and knew it, but this other, he'd done nothing and he was a book-learned man, a rabbi, not the same as the like of them, but for all that the Romans had done this to him. And maybe—maybe—it was a chance anyhow—"Rabbi!" he said, "Lord!" and saw that the one on the middle cross was listening. "I believe you're That One, yes I do! Remember me when you come to your kingdom!" He got his answer in a voice that had already lost strength: "Today—it will be today—I promise you shall be with me in Paradise." But the other bandit yelled with derision and anger and pain and began to sing a rather filthy song that was going round Jerusalem.

The centurion asked one of the soldiers what the man on the middle cross had said. It was getting unpleasantly dark now, another of these sandstorms. The soldier repeated it. "Very strange," said the centurion, "to go on believing in himself—even like this."

"A man that's dedicated, he'll go on thinking that way. Like we wouldn't give up our Eagles, sir, not if they was to cut us into little pieces!"

"Yes," said the centurion, "yes. But it's easier to die

fighting." He glanced at the drawn face of the one on the middle cross.

"Nor we wouldn't betray our comrades, sir, whatever was to be done to us."

"And he, I suppose, he feels some way he wouldn't betray his God. You know, I've seen some of these Jews dying for their God. But this man—it's not that, we weren't against his God. That wouldn't be sensible—not in Judæa anyway. I can't make out what it's all about."

"But he said he was the Son of God, sir! Making out he was some way equal to the Emperor. . . ."

"Oh yes," said the centurion with a snap, "that can't be allowed, of course." Best not to mention the Divine Emperor, even. Might lead to—politics.

.   .   .   .   .

The storm darkened over Jerusalem; for a time the sun could be seen through the clouds looking chill as a moon; then even that went. The shutters went up over the shops, though they were full enough with people buying in their last extras before Passover. Mothers screamed shrilly to their children to come in out of the streets and the children went running home, scared and crying. In the old Palace Barsiné fastened the shutters and drew the heavy curtains in the windows facing south-east, while some of the men slaves fastened in the glass window which Lady Claudia took about with her. Barsiné covered up the bed with its beautiful rugs and embroidered cover, and then the best of the chairs; another girl was bringing big sheets of linen and another rolling up the rugs; that would save them from the horrible desert sand that would be sure to come in on this wind, was just waiting to drop on them out of the dark, dirty-coloured clouds.

But Lady Claudia and her visitor paid little attention to this fussing. Madame Joanna was in tears, hardly able to speak. "I sent the message," Lady Claudia said to her. "I put it as strongly as I could, but . . ."

"The others were stronger," Joanna said.

"I suppose so," said Claudia, but secretly she thought that perhaps her husband had paid no attention, just thought she was meddling.

"They were all against him," Joanna said, "even the ones that were shouting for him five days ago. And they'll be sorry again tomorrow. But it will be too late. Too late! And then they'll hate your administration for letting them get their own way. It wasn't only the Sadducees, Lady Claudia, though they were the leaders. It was the Amharetz, the common people, the ones he loved! How could they?"

"Hasn't it happened before?" Lady Claudia said, "with the Gracchi—and Agis? So long as the common people have no—no philosophy, no education if you like—they will always turn on the ones who try to help them."

"He gave himself—for them," said Joanna, "and he was right. And it is our fault that they do the things that they do. How can they believe in brotherhood when they see—this?" And suddenly, shockingly, she tore one of the golden bracelets off her wrist and let it fall with a little crash on the floor. "This will go on until we are in full brotherhood," she said. "No rich. No poor. All of us the same under the new Promise."

"It seems a beautiful idea," said Lady Claudia, trying to comfort the other woman, but not really understanding what she was thinking or to what she was looking forward.

"He never thought you—you Romans—were any worse than the rest of the rich," said Madame Joanna, embarrassingly. "Some people held it against him. He'd talk to the tax collectors who work for you. They seem to be tainted to most people. I would try to speak to one—now— as if he were a friend. But it would still be an effort. They said he did it naturally, so he couldn't be a patriot."

"Really? How stupid!" said Lady Claudia. But the other woman went on without seeming to notice.

9—BYK

"All that has been brought up—on purpose—by his enemies and repeated. That way, the High Priest thinks he can keep on the right side of the mob, who call themselves patriots. He thinks he is on your right side already. And on the Tetrarch's."

"I never liked him!" said Claudia, and then wondered if she ought to have said it.

"No. No. Caiaphas only cared for power. He couldn't see the Kingdom. He couldn't understand what it meant, nor that it was beautiful. And our Jesus is dying now so as to show us—" said Joanna—"to show us that the Kingdom can go on without him being there. And we must follow him— even to death."

Claudia reached over and took Madame Joanna's hand in hers and patted it; a tear splashed warm on to her. "Perhaps," she said, hunting for words that might have some meaning to the other woman, "perhaps your friend's teaching—and it seems to me to be noble as far as I can understand it—will go on."

"Yes, yes. But how will it be without him? It is as if I were losing a beloved son. So often—I have tried to shelter him— after he had been giving himself out, teaching or healing; he was so easily hurt. And now . . ."

"It will be over soon," said Lady Claudia, as strongly as she could. What an extraordinary position to find oneself in, thinking like this of a condemned criminal!

.   .   .   .   .

In the Temple, too, the wind had sent people home; it had caught up all kinds of mess from the stalls, feathers and leaves, and here and there an odd scrap of scrawled parchment from a money-changer's stall. Some of the servants were told sharply to stop all this blowing through into the inner courts; they ran, tucking the ends of their head scarves down under their coats, glancing uneasily at the sky. Caiaphas said to his brother-in-law: "We'll have to have *that* over before the Sabbath." It was quite clear what he meant by *that*.

The other nodded: "Possibly orders might be given to have it expedited. If it could be explained at top level, what a bad impression it would produce. Don't you think so?"

"I hope so. The Roman is not making things easy for us."

"Possibly he knows that we might not—in certain eventualities—make things easy for him. After all, they are, when all's said and done, the enemy." He glanced at the Antonia fortress. "Threatening us. How easy it would be . . ." He shivered, thinking of what one order would do: the soldiers tramping in, ignoring the barriers, up to the altar itself. . . . Naturally, they would all die in its defence, but it might be useless.

Caiaphas brought him back to the actualities of the situation. "I have an idea that Pilate may, at the moment, not find me—shall we say?—the most congenial company. Will you go and ask to have their legs broken? That usually brings on death quite quickly."

"Very well. This storm—I have never known a day get so dark. I hope we have everything secured. The curtain . . ."

"Yes, I was thinking of that." Caiaphas went with long strides to the back of the altar. How beautiful it was, the great curtain, the veil of the Holy Place, of woven linen and wool, with all the colours of sea and sky and all the signs of the Angels. Whenever he looked at it Caiaphas felt the same quickening of his heart and catch in his breath: there was no heathen temple, not even in Rome itself, that had this beauty. Yet already this one, which was three years old, had begun to wear, with wind and rain in winter, and worse, the bleaching of the summer sun. It had lost its first magnificence. Yet there was another one in preparation; the dyeing was all finished and now the wives and daughters of one of the great Jerusalem families—cousins of his own—were busy on the weaving. It would be their gift.

.   .   .   .   .

By now there were hot bursts of sand coming with the wind; no way to start the Sabbath. Some of the crowd round the crosses had gone off home. "What time is it?" whispered the young Mary.

"About the time of the afternoon prayer," John whispered back, "but it's so dark. I can't see his face properly. I can't see if he is suffering. Almost—I've almost lost him. . . ."

"He has said nothing—for so long."

"He has scarcely moved. I think," said John, "he is deep inside himself, far away from us, and near to—near to——"

And then the voice came, not any longer the voice they knew, but high and shaken like the voice of a lost, hurt child. The voice said: "My God, my God, why have you forsaken me?" And then it died out into a painful sobbing. There was some whispering now among those standing round, watching this cross; the rumour had got about that there might, after all, be some miracle, some magic. Perhaps this was the moment. But the sick sobbing died down and the same thin voice muttered that it was thirsty. His mother gave a horrible start and dug her fingers into John's shoulder. Not to be able to do this for him . . . but one of the men reached up the sponge that had the drug on it, dipped, this time, into the vinegary cheap wine the soldiers had with them.

The darkness and oppression of the sand cloud seemed to be centrally over them now. John took a step forward, leaving the women. He had to be nearer, had to see. The head was beginning to drop now, as with intense tiredness; everything sagged and dropped, breath barely came. Then the head lifted a little, the eyelids flickered. The voice was only a whisper but it was recognisably the old voice that John knew to his bones. "It is finished," it said, and there was a strange small happiness in it, as though at last the mind were beginning to dissociate from the body and its pain. Then came a cry of breath tearing its way out, and then a low mutter, the last words that a good Jew says, the formal words that bring the spirit safe out of the body, scarcely audible, only a sentence coming through to the watchers: "Father, into thy hands I commend my spirit." And the head dropped completely and there was no more movement of any kind.

Sixteen

THERE must have been a moment of intense quiet. John, turning, was aware of it, and then all at once, seeing his face, a wailing broke out of the three women and was taken up by others; only a wailing, no disturbance, no anger, but intense and shattering grief, so that the centurion found himself oddly disquieted, feeling that something had happened out of the run of ordinary crucifixions. However, the other two were still alive, and here was a message saying they were to be polished off and got out of the way before the end of the afternoon. "On account of this feast of theirs," said the centurion, "though why they should fuss—— Hullo, what the hell was that?" For the ground under his feet had given a perceptible and unpleasant shake, sending him off balance for a moment.

"Only a small earthquake, sir," said the soldier next him; "always having these earthquakes. Why, I remember in Gerasa——"

"Well, I hope we haven't done anything to upset the gods," said the centurion surprisingly.

"What, over *him*, sir? Not likely! Look, the sky's clearing. These sandstorms drive me scatty." But the centurion still looked worried.

The soldiers went over and did what was necessary to the two bandits, who howled for a minute or two and then, as the blood began to pour out of the arteries in their smashed legs, fell into moaning, whispered prayers and silence. Just to make sure, someone stuck a spear in between the ribs at heart level on the man who hung on the middle cross. But,

as he had supposed, that one was dead. It only fetched a bit
more upset from the women, of whom there seemed to be
quite a few now, and some respectable-looking ones among
them.

John Priest left them and went over to the brothers. "You
came back, James," he said.

"Yes," said James, "I came back. And now I am taking a
solemn vow before you and my brother Simon that I shall
neither eat nor drink until I speak again with my brother
Jesus."

"You mean . . ." said John.

"Yes," said James, "that is what I mean." Both of them
turned and looked at the crosses and the dead bodies.

John wiped his sleeve across his face; everything seemed
to be gritty with sand. He had not even noticed the slight
shake and shock of the earth. Nor had the women, already
so shaken by their own grief. "I wonder what they mean to
do with them?" he said.

"What does it matter?" said James. "It is only a body
now." But John could not think of it like that. He stood
there, wondering if he ought to do something and yet for the
moment not able to set his mind even. on to what it ought
to be. Simon was looking as if he had been knocked on the
head. He couldn't, anyhow, pull himself together nor make
sense of what James had said.

.   .   .   .   .

The earthquake had not done much damage. Here and
there a jar had been tipped over or a basket upset from a
shelf; one or two roofs were down. But it had loosened a
stone in the lintel of the great doorway to the inner place.
Coming down, the stone had torn the Veil of the Temple in
one corner. But the new one was half woven already, or
should have been. Caiaphas was ordering the servants to
clear away the débris; the lintel stone could be mortared
back into place.

"That one is dead," said Eleazar.

"I feel a new man, cleansed and strengthened!" said Caiaphas, and opened his arms. "Sabbath is coming, true gold, and there is the sun shining again below the clouds!"

"All the same I wish he had not made that prophecy about the Temple," his friend said. "It is terrible to think that all this might have an ending."

"He may have said that out of sheer spite and enmity," said Caiaphas, "or he may have meant that there was sin in the building since it was old Herod's work. True enough. Though I do not suppose Herod escaped hell because of it." He added lower: "If there is such a place. Yet all that has been burnt and purified out of it, by ourselves and the meaning of what we do. I see the Temple as the centre of the world; yes, I see it as a great humming-top, turning and blurring, so fast that it seems not to move, ever changing yet ever still, and ourselves driving it!"

"Be careful," said his friend urgently, "that is pride—spiritual pride. . . ."

Caiaphas looked at him, then round at the tower of the Antonia and the little moving figures of the soldiers on the parapet, then back to the bits of stone which had been knocked out by the earthquake and now lay at his feet, the bright new-broken surface exposed to the sun. "Yes," he said, "my besetting sin, I'm afraid. And, for that matter, what *he* died of. You know, by the end I really hated him. Yes, he set himself up against the Temple, whether he intended to do so originally, or not. All this preaching in synagogues. Even as things are, the synagogues and the argument and hair-splitting that goes on in them distract people's minds from the central realities . . . here. And if that Nazarene had got his way, it might have started a landslide."

"I see what you mean. That phrase of his which caught on about a temple not made with hands: it might have encouraged men to pray anywhere!"

"Exactly. Well, I think I must go and speak to the maidens about hurrying on the new Veil. I have just time before Sabbath begins. These well-born ones are lazier than slaves."

.   .   .   .   .

His Excellency had now finished his lunch, and had had a nice snooze in congenial female company which he kept at the Antonia so as to avoid any awkwardness. He was on his way to the first main of the cock-fight. He needed a little stimulation, a spot of noise and blood and general interest. The message from the priests asking to have the condemned men finished off before the Passover Sabbath had come during his nice snooze, and Gaius Crispus had thought it more sensible not to disturb H.E. but to send the order down in his name. One had sometimes to make these decisions. If disturbed, H.E. might well have refused to oblige the priests' party. Which might have had serious consequences: for himself and possibly for his staff. Now the message came through that the criminals were all dead and that the crucifixion guard party was having the bodies taken down. "Good, good," said the Procurator, "now that's out of the way."

The cock-fights were going to be held in the paved courtyard of the Antonia, next to the stones with the marks for the dice game. There were convenient steps for the spectators to sit on, just as in Rome. A certain amount of wine had already gone round, and the soldiers cheered H.E. in a rather undisciplined way and even clapped him on the back; two or three of them began singing a song which referred to certain of his physical powers and suggested means of demonstrating them. Officially he took no cognisance of the song, but still it was all quite gratifying; much better to be popular with one's own fellows! Good old din they were making. That lot in the Temple would be praying away like mad, yowling and mooing with those crazy towels over their heads: no doubt they would hear the Antonia's answer to prayer!

Hector felt that he could safely leave the Old Man now; it was much pleasanter to be somewhere right away from him where one could bet and spit and generally behave like a free man. He had been over to see Esdras during the lunch break. Esdras had been all to bits and said this man who was being crucified was Messiah. What did he mean by that? These Jews were so extraordinary; you supposed they were rational people with the same ideas as yourself—Esdras spoke excellent Greek—and then out would come something that was quite meaningless to anyone with any genuine philosophy. He wondered if Madame Joanna had managed to say anything helpful to Lady Claudia about what her husband was doing.

The Procurator sat on the steps with his knees straddled apart; this was a strictly male gathering where one could sit at ease and scratch. He'd had a report in about the head of the taxation department at Jericho, a little gold-mine of a place, all that irrigation, two or three crops a year. This man used to be good: chap called Zacchæus. Seems he'd started giving money away, burning I.O.U.s and generally behaving as if he was off his head. Well, he'd have to be dealt with. There were plenty more who'd like his job, even if they accused him of Romanising in public! Absent-mindedly he began to do sums in his head. Nice to think of the money coming in. The boy might need a bit, now he was starting out in life. At his age, thought Pontius Pilate, I still thought a woman was something special; nearly made a fool of myself once or twice. The boy's scarcely started shaving yet, but there, if he takes after his dad . . . And there was the girl's dowry too; he'd like the wedding to go with a splash when he was in Rome, as he intended to be, later on in the year. But the cocks were circling round one another now, the feathers standing out well. One made a spring, was parried. Yes, at the eyes! Both sprang, everyone was shouting at them.

Ah, nice bit of work! Besides, it was a pleasure to lift even a small bet on a cock-fight off young Gaius.

. . . . .

The slaves at the Residence brought bowls of water and cloths and went over the marble floors quickly, getting rid of the dust that the storm had left. Barsiné drew the curtains again, shook them, and looked round at her lady. Terrible that she should have been so worried by Madame Joanna. She hadn't recovered her spirits yet, just sat there drooping. "His Excellency is not back yet?" she asked once. Barsiné shook her head. "When he does come, word is to go to him that—oh, he is to be asked is it convenient for him to receive me?" Yes, thought Barsiné, she's at arm's-length there, and no wonder. Perhaps if the musicians were to come and play something in the courtyard, something light and gay—but Lady Claudia was quite cross, scolded Barsiné, who fell at her feet and kissed them. Then, worse and worse, Lady Claudia began to cry.

Barsiné jumped up and began fussing over her, brought wine, brought fruit, brought a fold of linen steeped in cold water to lay on her forehead. Lady Claudia dabbed her eyes, stopped and smiled at Barsiné. "Child," she said, "tell me something about yourself. Can you remember when you were quite little? Were you free?"

Barsiné's face suddenly sparkled; her lady had shown favour, was speaking about herself! Yet it was difficult to find the Greek words; she talked plenty of Greek, had spoken nothing else since—whenever it was—but the time before that was not in Greek. "We were in a little town, my mistress," she said, "and I played with my sisters. Then there was fighting. My big sister was killed," she said, and her eyes clouded over because she had seen it and it was horrible and now she was being asked to remember it.

"And so you were carried off?" Lady Claudia asked.

"Yes. And they whipped me. And took off all my own

clothes and threw them away. And I was tied for a long time. And I had to walk, walk."

"Where did you go?"

"It was some great city. I never knew. Perhaps it had a name. And then I had to learn to speak. When I said the old words, then they whipped me."

"Poor child!"

"But, my mistress, if I could only speak the old, stupid way, nobody would want me. So I learnt to speak the new words and to sing and to sew quick—quick—and to be good, and then my mistress wanted me. So it was all well."

"Do you ever wonder about the gods, Barsiné? Did you have any gods of your own?" Barsiné shook her head; she had forgotten what gods she used to have. "You do not believe in this god of the Jews here?"

"No," said Barsiné, "my Lady's gods are my gods."

"What would you do if you were free, Barsiné?"

She looked a little dreamy, at last said: "I think, maybe, someone would want me—to be a wife for him."

"So you wouldn't be free, even then," said Claudia, half to herself, then said: "Well, some day, Barsiné, we will marry you to some good man and I will give you a dowry."

"But not now!" said Barsiné passionately, and caught her mistress round the knees. "I want to belong to my mistress! You are not angry with stupid Barsiné? No?"

She gazed up at Claudia, who laughed: "No, no, I'm not angry!" And stooped quickly and kissed Barsiné on the forehead.

Seventeen

THE cock-fighting had gone wonderfully. His Excellency was feeling in grand form again. So when Hector came to tell him that one of the priests was asking for an audience there was no immediate come-back of anger, but the curious expression of shrewdness that Hector knew well and which was quite impressive appeared on his face. "Not one of *those*?" he said.

"No, sir," said Hector, "the other party, the Pharisees, the strict ones."

"Funny," said the Procurator, "I wouldn't have thought one of that lot would have come here—" and he looked round the paved court and smelt good Roman sweat and a bit of blood to salt it, even if it were only cock's blood—"just when this feast of theirs is on."

"Those ones kept it last night, I think, sir," said Hector; "something to do with this Sabbath of theirs."

"Wonder what he wants? M'm. Get my toga, Hector. Look sharp. I think I'll go to the gate and have a word with him. Need to stretch my legs anyway. Come along, Gaius!" he shouted. "Divide and rule, what!"

. . . . .

Joseph of Arimathæa waited at the gate. He was not at all certain that the Procurator would grant his request; he had not wanted to ask him for anything, nor even to go near his fortress, least of all on the Sabbath Eve. The very look of the place, huge and menacing and cruel, was a threat to his peace of mind, his certainty in being one of Israel, the chosen people. Yet, this Sabbath, had he peace of mind? Was not the golden Sabbath Eve shattered and lying in pieces round him? All his life he had hoped for Messiah; it had seemed from month to month that the prophecies of time and history were being fulfilled. Then word had come that in Galilee of the old songs, Galilee of the folded hills and the great blue lake, there was a boy growing up. A son had been born to Israel. Time went on and word began to come back to Jerusalem; it was talked over in the courts of the Temple and the houses of the rabbis. The boy in Galilee was growing up. He, in his person, was fulfilling the other prophecies, those of the doings of the man.

It was spoken about by Joseph and his friends, more and more often. Because, if this were true, if this were indeed the certain and final Master of Righteousness, then nothing else mattered. But at first the whole thing had seemed impossible; when something has been dreamed over for so many centuries it is too much to believe that the dream may become actual. The Pharisees had sent to try him, sent their wisest and most learned, and at first they had supposed that the whole thing was an imposture: he was, after all, only a carpenter's son from a small village. He had stood up to preach in the synagogue of his own place and they had thought ill of him. Nor did he welcome the learned with deference, but instead went off, cheerful and laughing at them, with a few common fishermen, or women, or, worse, the Romanisers, even those who had defiled themselves by tax-collecting for the army of occupation, the lowest of the low, doing their masters' dirty work. Nor were there the signs that Messiah might or should have had, the floating glory, the Cherubim at last visible to all eyes behind his head. Yet there had been something about him. Nicodemus was the first who had clearly seen it. He had come back and told them that this Jesus of Nazareth must, for certain, have had some kind of experience which put him into a special position with regard to God.

They had talked it over, were talking it over still. But they had decided that he ought to be protected in case, or until, his time came. They had sent him warnings. He had not chosen to heed them. They had been in touch with young John, his follower, although John had been brought up in the other party, to which he was born. But they had not made up their minds as a body or, indeed, as individuals. Except that, when challenged, Nicodemus had said he believed that Jesus of Nazareth was Messiah. And he himself, had he said that? Yes, what else could he say against the violence and tyranny of Caiaphas and his party?

But was it true? Was he the Messiah, the Chosen One who had come to save Israel? And, if so, what had Israel done?

So he stood there, turning it over in his mind, and suddenly the Roman was standing in front of him in the gateway, looking exceedingly official but at least serious. The most terrible thing was when the Romans laughed with their great open, stinking mouths and you couldn't tell what they were laughing at. Joseph bowed. "Can I do anything to help you?" said the Procurator, with something like amiability.

"Why—yes, Your Excellency," said Joseph. "I have come to ask for the body of one of those who was crucified today."

"Ah yes," said the Procurator, "the one who was called King, no doubt."

"It is that one."

"I would gladly have released him," said the Procurator, conversationally, "at the time of your feast. I had it in mind to do so, but apparently . . ." He shrugged his shoulders.

"Caiaphas and his father-in-law Annas who hated him had that arranged!" said Joseph. "If we had known in time . . ."

"A pity, wasn't it? I would of course have been happy to oblige your party, for whom I have a great respect. For my own part, I could not see that the poor fellow had done anything deserving of death."

Was the Roman being serious? You couldn't tell. "I may go and take the body, then, Your Excellency?"

"Certainly. So long as you do not use it to create a disturbance."

"I propose," said Joseph, "to have the body decently wrapped and then laid in my own family tomb."

"One of these rock affairs, I take it?"

"Yes. It is cut out of the rock. There is a stone that rolls across the entrance. It can be sealed for ever. I have a garden planted in front of it."

"Ah yes, very nice," said the Procurator, "very suitable. Hector, write an order." He wrote it and the Procurator sealed in into the wax with his ring. "Take this to the centurion in charge of the crucifixion party and he will let you have the body. I am delighted to have been of service to you."

There were some formal leave-takings, then Joseph of Arimathæa hurried away, carrying the tablet. Let him get the body first before it was thrown into a ditch or whatever nastiness the soldiers might do. Once that was safe he would get the wrappings and whatever else was necessary and arrange to have it carried to the tomb.

"That was clever of you, sir," said Gaius admiringly; "can't do any harm, and might do a lot of good."

"Yes," said the Procurator; "if that other lot go complaining to Rome, this lot are going to defend me. Equally, if the Sadducees try to set the mob on me when they turn round and see what they've done, the Pharisees will have a good report. It's turned out very conveniently. Here—" he flung off his toga and threw it at Hector—"you take this away. I don't propose to miss any more of the fun."

    .   .   .   .   .

The centurion recognised the seal, saluted and gave a quick order. One of the men, with a few hammer taps under the head, got the nails out. Straightened, they'd do again for

another crucifixion; in fact it was seldom that they had to go
to the expense of new nails, though the old ones had to be
sharpened occasionally. The body tumbled off the wood on
to the rocks, the neck loose, the blood dry on hands and feet.
Flies rose off it.

Joseph beckoned young John over. "Keep watch," he
said, "I am going now for the wrappings. The Roman
agreed."

"Without making difficulties?"

"None at all. Only that there should be no disturbance.
How could there be—now?"

"Yes," said John, "he is quiet. Oh, how quiet he is."

Joseph went back through the city with the sun tilting
westward towards the Sabbath. And prayer rising from men's
hearts into the sky, wherever a few men of Israel were
gathered together. The things he needed were in his town
house; he called a servant and unlocked a chest. Here, in
stoppered jars, were certain vegetable compounds which
would keep a body temporarily from decay. There was no
time before the Sabbath was on them to rub in the precious
ointments which he would have liked to use. He would give
some to the women and they could come back on the day
after Sabbath and deal with the body. Perhaps they would
want to take it back to Galilee; he might lend them an
ox cart.

He had bought these compounds for his own family use if
need were. He took them out and asked his wife for a new
web of linen. She brought it and looked at the jars, troubled.
"You are taking them?" "Yes," said her husband, "I have
need." She shook her head; it was not a wife's part to ask; a
wife must save and her husband spend. One day she would
find out.

He put the jars into a basket and himself carried the linen.
As he went out he said to the doorkeeper: "If Nicodemus
comes, tell him—I am gone to bury Messiah." What did he
mean, the doorkeeper wondered?—some kind of wise words

with a meaning hidden. He memorised them and told
Nicodemus when he came.

He was not the only one to wonder. Joseph of Arimathæa
was well known. Several people greeted him but got nothing
back. He seemed to be deeply preoccupied. And why was he,
in his own arms, carrying what appeared to be shrouding
cloth? It seemed out of tune with the evening. For most
people in Jerusalem the sense of Sabbath and Passover was
strong, the knowledge of their own God who had delivered
them out of Egypt, who might yet deliver them from
another bondage! Butchers and bakers, builders' labourers,
from the palace down to the back yards of the Ophel, they
were all glad and proud and there were good words on
their lips.

Even the Tetrarch, Herod Antipas, was now looking
forward to the Sabbath candles. Sometimes he disliked being
in Jerusalem, preferring his own northern tetrarchy, where
he did not have Romans watching him, Romans who had
taken his own father's palace away from him so that he had
to pretend to be content with the older one which had
belonged to the dynasty which his own family had finished
off. He disliked being asked to the Residence by the Romans,
so strong a feeling had he that it was really his own. But no
Roman had the Sabbath—that belonged only to one people.

Eighteen

(*5 to 6 p.m.*)

JOSEPH of Arimathæa was kneeling over the body, trying not to think too much about what he was doing.

The two old ones had come over and were helping him. It was better to do the thing here on the ground, not waste time taking it to a house. Nobody would want to have a crucified body in any room of theirs, so near the Sabbath too. There was no time to take it to his own house, even if it were the body of the Messiah. If that were so, and if he had been murdered, they would need to begin again with the old waiting and watching. Until God bethought him again of mankind. Thinking this, he handled the body, washing the worst away, so that the women could rub the limp limbs with the compounds, touching the dear flesh once more before it was lost for ever. The mother was murmuring to herself—what? Pet names from childhood they must have been, little lamb, little dove. Joseph of Arimathæa turned his head away, not wanting to hear. It was not fitting for a man to weep.

He spoke occasionally to John, who, himself, was working dazedly, sometimes looking at his own hands, reddened by his teacher's blood. In a while Nicodemus came, bowed and made old by grief, waving his hands despairingly. "Once more," he said, "once more the children of light are defeated!"

And the young woman, what was happening to her? She sat on a rock, her head bowed on her knees and her arms over her head, her hands clasped and twisted across it. She should have been helping! "Come, Mary!" said Salome sharply, "we all feel the same, my girl, but there's work to do." Jerkily the hands unfolded themselves, the head shifted. And the eyes looked past, past, not recognising any of them.

John stood up and went over. "Mary," he said, "what is it?" But she shrank away from him as though, John felt, he had made some filthy gesture at her. "Mother," he said, "you speak to her."

The old Mary turned, and, as she did so, the limp, swollen and yet bloodless hand which she had been holding fell off her lap. And it seemed as though that was the one thing which the young woman was looking at, for suddenly she screamed, a horrible, echoing kind of screaming that made the soldiers jump. It went on as though she had no need to take breath, with a noise in the throat that made it twice as bad. The centurion came over: "What's all this? Tell that girl to stop it!"

"I am afraid," said John Priest, "all this has taken her reason away—she was like this once before. He cured her."

"Well, he can't cure her now," said the centurion. "Stop it, girl, or I'll smack your face." She didn't stop, only her one cheek reddened and flared where the smack had landed. She had not seemed to notice it. Old Salome got up. "I'll take her home," she said, "then I'll come back."

"Come to my garden," said Joseph, "it will be best to have—watchers." And he gave her careful instructions so that she could get there, even after dark.

Salome took the young Mary's arm and pulled her to her feet; she was screaming less, or rather the screaming had lost volume, had become a kind of wordless whimper. Two of the other women from the Ophel Quarter came with her. "Yes," said Salome, "her devils have come back into the poor thing. And it looks like they'll be there for keeps now."

But the others were wrapping the body, so that now it was all covered except the face, which had been smoothed and calmed and now seemed almost to be asleep. His mother was bending over, kissing it and dropping tears on to it, but already the skin was chill and strange. John Priest took the head and Simon, his brother, the feet; they lifted and began to carry. Joseph led the way, looking back from time to time over his shoulder. Nicodemus followed, lamenting to himself, then a few of the men. One of them had gone to the house of someone he knew, got charcoal in a pot and a few torches. It would be dark before they had finished. Then came the mother and some other women with her, not wailing very loudly.

The garden had a fairly high stone wall round it, with a locked wooden door. Joseph unlocked it and they followed him in, quickly; the sun was almost down. John wondered what had been done with the other two bodies, all smashed up as they were; he had forgotten to look but perhaps their friends had taken them. It was against Jewish law to leave the body of an executed criminal unburied after nightfall. A merciful law as compared with other nations, where tortured, dying creatures might hang on stakes or half burnt or speared on to a door for nights and days. And on a Sabbath night it was most needful of all. If nobody came for them the guards might toss them into some old well.

Meanwhile here for them was the end of the road: a square hole in the rock—empty. Gently they slid in the thing they were carrying. There was a kind of shelf at the back, where a body could lie full length. One of the torches had been lit. Now that it lay so, it seemed sleeping; they spoke in whispers, as though beside some dreaming friend. The mother came into the tomb and stooped over while John held the torch. She too went out. It was dusk now; the Sabbath had begun. But there was one thing more to do. "This," said Joseph, "is a work of necessity." And he pointed at the stone. It rolled in a groove, a great heavy thing like a huge mill-stone. John and Simon pushed at it, but could do nothing at all until all the rest came. Then with some lifting slightly and others pushing, the thing moved, rolled over ponderously and noisily and shut off the tomb.

"I will keep the first watch " his mother said; "there are things I have to remember."

"Shall I wait?" John asked.

She shook her head: "Go back and find the others. They will want to know—everything. Salome will come. Nobody will hurt two old women."

"I'll stay with you, Mother," said Simon. As usual nobody paid any attention to him. But he stayed, sitting on a stone a little way off.

One by one they went out of the gate. Joseph of Arimathæa handed Mary the key before leaving himself. Nobody said anything. There seemed to be nothing left to say. Only an emptiness in the heart. As they came back through the gate and into the city they began to hear the singing of psalms and, wherever there was a window only half shuttered, to see the golden light of the Sabbath candles shining on the clean linen spread over the table.

Nineteen

IN the Ophel the news was going round. Somebody told Jesus bar Rabban in the house where he was keeping Passover: this Passover he had so desperately wanted to have with his own gang, the patriots who'd been with him at the Tower. And now here they were together. Not all. Poor Malachi bar Joses, dead that very day. He hadn't made out yet what had been happening, what fighting he'd been killed in. But it was the blasted Romans again, the oppressors, always picking off the good ones. But one day—one day—he'd need to get his forces together again. They were scattered over the country now, but they'd come together yet, the patriots, who'd get rid of the Romans and the Romanisers at one go. Somebody told him that Caiaphas, the High Priest, had encouraged his folk, told them to keep on shouting and they'd get him released and he, Caiaphas, he'd do what he could, on the inside like, to help. Now, what did that mean? Did the priest's party think they could buy him up? If they did they were wrong.

And this poor chap who'd just been crucified, he'd been a patriot in his way, only not practical. It took a man from the city to be practical. These Galileans, always singing and talking—and good fighters too when it came to the point; but they couldn't organise. So, he was dead. Another score to settle with the Romans. And once dead, he'd be forgotten.

For a time Jesus bar Rabban and his friends were lost in the ritual, the singing of the psalms, the drinking of the cups, the opening of the door for Messiah—how long to wait now? But I and my lot, we'll be the first to welcome him, he thought, and Messiah will see how we've struggled for Israel and reward us when his kingdom comes. He thought then about these Galileans; would he be able to recruit them? If so, now might be the time. He spoke to one of his friends, who said it wouldn't be much use, considering the mess-up about this leader of theirs who seemed to have gone mad, and had walked straight back into the hands of the ones who were after him.

"Most likely they tortured him, made all kinds of threats; I know them," said Bar Rabban. "One's got to be as tough as they are to come through. I'll go myself and have a talk to his crowd." So, when the meal was finished, he and one or two of his men went over to the house where they thought they could find the Galileans. It was dark now, though the moon was rising on the other side of the hills beyond the valley, beyond the Mount of Olives and Bethany, so that the sky above them was luminous, a very deep, very distant blue. But so much of the Ophel was a maze of narrow streets, with windows jutting out above them, and steps, up and down the hill, that they were often in pitch darkness. One of the men had a torch, but it was wonderful for Bar Rabban to be free again, feeling his way through his own dirty, beloved Jerusalem, picking up the old familiar smells, the feel of the walls, cold after sundown but with the crumbly friendly feeling of mud bricks, not the harsh stone of prisons.

They came to the house and knocked; no answer, so they knocked again. After a while an old woman came to the door and opened it a few inches, asking suspiciously what they wanted. "I want to speak to your men," said Bar Rabban. She shook her head, saying there was nobody there, only a few women and a poor, sick girl. "Nonsense," said Bar Rabban and got his foot into the door. "I want to see them, and they'll want to see me." One of his men suddenly leant his weight on the door, pushing it and the old woman backward into the room. Another woman screamed at them, but they paid no attention to that. In the dim light of a single-wicked lamp in the wall they had seen what looked like the men they wanted.

One of them jumped to his feet. "Who's that?" he asked in his strong Galilean accent.

"We are patriots," said Bar Rabban. "Look—I know who you are. And I'm giving you the chance to join us. We know who killed your leader. Blood for blood. Are you on?"

"Don't answer him, Flash!" said one of the others. "Let them go their way. We go ours."

"What's your way, after all?" said Bar Rabban. "Aren't we going the same way? To get the Romans out of Israel. To clean our country of the Romanisers and the priests that eat up the goods and lives of the ordinary people—you and me. Oh, I know what your leader, peace be on him, said about them!"

"You've got it wrong," said Flash heavily. "We've got to change them and forgive them, not kill them."

"Much good it'll do you trying to change that crowd!" said Bar Rabban. "You've tried—haven't you? And failed. They didn't care. They'll crucify the lot of you, then you'll be finished. Whereas if you join up with me, we'll get somewhere."

"Get out," said another man from the back of the room, without moving.

"I'm not getting out till I make you see," said Bar Rabban. "Look—your way's proved useless. It hasn't done anything, only got your man killed. In spite of him being a good man, I'm not denying that. Try my way. Surely you aren't going to let him go unrevenged?"

"God our Father will take care of that. If it is in his Will," said Flash. "For us: we have to forgive." And he suddenly sobbed. It seemed to come out of his stomach, as though the thought of it made him sick and yet he had to take it.

"Forgive! And you call yourselves men of Israel. Yes, and Galileans. There were Galileans before you that didn't talk like that—in the Gorge of Pigeons. . . ." He saw the man's fists clench; he hadn't liked that; no Galilean would. "And you let your leader die and be forgotten——"

"No!" said Flash. "He is God's son. We saw that! Ourselves—up on the hill. . . ."

"God's son! And you let him be crucified!"

Flash suddenly, in one movement, jumped to his feet and hit out with his right straight for Bar Rabban's jaw. It was another man who knocked his arm up, but it took all of them to hold him. All of them—and his brother.

"Stop it, Flash," said Stormy. "I know how you feel. But this is our temptation. See? See, Flash?"

Flash gulped. "Yes. Yes. My hand didn't touch him. I was trying to talk—to explain—to be patient. But it came over me. I didn't hit him, Stormy! No, I didn't. My hand was held."

"Yes, by the rest of us, young Flash!" said Stormy. 'We've got to do better than this. Haven't we, Rocky?"

"We have," said Rocky. "We've got to have his words working in us—in our living and doing, the whole time. And it's going to be hard. Harder than we ever thought. You're Bar Rabban, aren't you? Well, do you know this? It was you the crowd wanted, instead of our Jesus, the Son, the One Foretold. If it hadn't been for you, they might have taken him out of the hands of the Romans. But it was your way they chose, you—patriot! They turned their backs on the Kingdom of Heaven. They chose something to fight for. A power."

"Israel. Yours and mine."

"But if you can't choose both." Rocky was puzzling out his thought, slowly chiselling it out of the tough rock of his mind. "And maybe you can't. I don't know. It was their luck. They never heeded the prophets. They didn't choose

Messiah. The one that God chose. Only some of us, we saw farther. Because he showed us."

Stormy said: "We had to choose too. We'd got our folk, our girls, our boats. We were doing well. We threw it all up, for him. We don't ever want to make any other choice. Although now—it looks like we shall have to go back."

"I could do with you," Bar Rabban said once more, ignoring the older men and speaking directly to the young one. "A pity to waste a good strong fist like yours—even if it nearly knocked me out! I wouldn't offer you an easy life, but I can see you don't want that. You'd get fighting; that would put out the taste of the grief you're in and the shame you feel over what you've done—or not done. Don't tell me you're not ashamed; I can see it!"

"I'm ashamed, right enough," said Flash, "because I haven't got it in me to make you see that your way won't come to anything. But ours will. He could have made you see."

"He! He's dead! He'll be stinking soon." Bar Rabban spoke with a lash of contempt. They were no good, this crowd; gone soft.

"Make him go!" said Flash, and turned and beat his hands and head on the wall.

"Mad!" said Bar Rabban and turned on his heel. As they left, one of his men passed the girl who had screamed and who was now sitting on the floor, silent, twitching her fingers. He pulled her veil back and was going to have done plenty more, seeing that these Galileans wouldn't fight, but the girl let out with another scream that scared him out of what he'd been after. "Come on out!" said Bar Rabban, "we'll get no good out of this madhouse!" He was disappointed. They ought to have jumped at it. They were betraying their country's cause.

"Oh, Miss Mary, don't!" said Rocky, in a kind of despair. It was almost too much, now. And to know that there would be no more healing, no casting out of devils, and the pride and joy they themselves got out of it! Gradually the screaming died down and she fell back into the corner against the cushions with her eyes not quite shut, but an edge of white showing. "What can we do with her?" he said.

"We'll need to take her back with us to Magdala," Salome said.

"What will her father say?"

"It can't be helped what her father will say. There's nothing can be helped now, and the sooner you boys see that the better. The boats will still be there."

"I wish I was back," said Stormy, "in the boat, and a good day. The fish making in for the warm springs and my nets in good order. A bit of a ripple and the dark clouds running their shadows on the hills at the other side. Or coming on for evening, the rustle of the reeds going on all the time and the frogs beginning to croak. And us in our boat hearing it all and getting the smell of the land mixed in with the smell of the nets."

"The crying of the lambs on our own hills coming over the water."

"The streaks of snow on Hermon, right up in the sky. It was like that the day——"

"The day he called us. It's no good, Stormy. We can go back right enough, and maybe that's what we've got to do. But it'll all be mixed up with him and how he looked and what he said. We'll never be able to forget him."

"You talk as if you wanted to," said Rocky.

"I don't. I don't. Only I feel—lost. My shepherd's gone."

"You'll need to get used to it, boys," said Salome. "Now, I'm going off to the tomb to be company for poor Mary. There's two or three coming with me and we'll talk away about the old days. When the Sabbath's over we'll do everything that should be done and then we'll take that poor broken-up body of his back with us to Galilee. And I wish we'd never come to Jerusalem. Poor Mary, to walk all this way behind the little donkey and it loaded with good things for our cousins, and all for a sight of the boy. And at the end of it, all she sees is him on the cross." She was wrapping herself up as she spoke and filling a couple of flat pieces of bread with dried fish and onions and peppers. Eaten in the early morning it would keep the cold out of the watchers.

"And Miss Mary?" said Rocky.

"You'll need to do your best, Rocky, and that's all any of us can do. Try your hand on healing her!" she added unkindly. Big Rocky had done some bragging once or twice, and she hadn't forgotten it. She took a small lamp, filled it with oil and fitted in a wick. If she went slow it would stay alight outside; she shielded it with her hand as she opened the door and went off into the night, talking to herself for company.

Mary of Magdala had heard it all, but as though from the other side of a wall. The words were not real words; they were only sounds pretending to be words, they didn't get to her past the shapes that crowded and swung all round her, and the torn hand that kept falling past them, that couldn't keep them away. She began again to look at her own hands and move them here and there; they too seemed to be a long way off and the sharp red and purple very close to her eyes. She could see Rocky watching her. He couldn't see the shapes. If only he could. She tried to smile at him. No use.

· · · · ·

John Priest had come back. He stood against the wall, telling them, in a dead kind of voice, about Joseph of Arimathæa, who had managed to deal with the Romans. Otherwise—he shivered, thinking what might have been done with the body. Before that, Salome hadn't been able to tell them what had happened, only that they'd been given the body and now it was wrapped decently. This man who seemed to be giving orders—she hadn't known who he was. The head ones were always the same; only sometimes they were on your side. Just sometimes. Mostly they were against. But for John, Joseph bar Achim was not merely another rich man, but almost one of themselves, almost in the Kingdom. The others told him about how Bar Rabban had come and how they hadn't managed to answer him properly; the words wouldn't come, but they'd done their best. "I think," said John, "that maybe we shall understand better in a day or two."

Rocky looked at him hard: "Do you mean—something special?"

"I don't know!" said John. "I don't dare to guess! I saw him dead. Dead. We have to try and think what he meant when he came to Jerusalem."

"He meant to give Jerusalem a chance to choose him. And they chose Bar Rabban," said Rocky.

"He meant to show us something about the Kingdom," said Stormy, "but what?"

"The prophecies had to be fulfilled," said John slowly. "He always said that. I always thought of the prophecies as the branches of a tree, and he the living sap running through them and bursting out into blossom. But now I can't think clearly of them or him."

They stood for quite a long time, saying nothing. John was suddenly hungry. There was a pot of soured milk and some cooked beans in a bowl. He meant to eat some, but somehow couldn't face it. They all knew it was Sabbath, yet that meant nothing now. Nothing at all. Only a blank.

"I wonder where Judas is now?" Rocky said suddenly. "Not a trace of him."

"I'd like to think he'd hung himself!" Stormy said.

"That's too good for him!" said Flash. "I'd like him to fall on a sharp rock and his guts to spill out on to the ground

—and it would be hot—and I'd like him not to die at
once . . ."

"Ah, Father God!" said John, "what did he mean—what
did he mean?" But at the pain in his voice when he said
that the shapes advanced again on Mary, jangling all their
colours and forcing her to scream.

Twenty

"THAT'S over," Annas said to his son-in-law. Was he thinking about the Passover—one more Passover and peaceable enough, as things went, no real trouble from the pilgrims—or about the teacher who had, in fact, troubled them so much? The old man had had difficulties in his time, thought Caiaphas, but not quite this one.

There had been all this talk of Messiahs for as long back as anyone could remember. Whenever somebody turned up whose ideas were out of the common, people would be found to call him Messiah and to persuade him that this was what he was, though it had never before gone quite as far as this. It was, perhaps, a sign of great unhappiness, or at least discontent among the people. But how, after all, could a man be content if he was one of the Amharetz, the common people, doomed to work all his life and at the end find himself old with no more than a few days of happiness? If you did not think, never raised your head out of the mud into the clear air of reason and beauty, that could be done. But if once they start thinking, Caiaphas said to himself, they will begin to think about Messiahs. I would think like that if I were one of them. But praise be to the Lord God, I am not. So I do not need to have these wild thoughts, nor to see visions. He made some amiable remark to old Annas, whom he held in esteem.

One day Israel would be a great nation again, conquering and gathering in; that was her proud destiny. Rome would crumble. How else, with a morality worse than the dogs? There was no coherence of family life, no worship in the sense that it should be understood, but a mass of superstition and idols; their women were allowed an intolerable licence and went about so that you could not tell a wife from a harlot. Yet for the moment Rome had the power, and power was a thing which must be approached with the utmost care and even deference. Well, in the long run the Procurator and his power would lose over today's doings. It had been in some ways very unpleasant; but mostly because of the moment when he had caught himself believing that there was something in it. It would be some time before he could forget that he had experienced that feeling.

Annas said: "That boy John; we shall have to do something about him."

"Which John?" said Caiaphas, puzzled.

"The one who has been going about with this Jesus of Nazareth. I am not happy about him. After all, he is a relation. And the time might come when he could be called to service in the Temple. The rest of the man's followers will doubtless be scattered. Most of them are country people; they will go back to work, marry, grow old, and have some queer tales for their grandchildren. But John is different; it might affect him very badly. I should not like him to become in any way eccentric."

"Perhaps the marriage canopy is the best remedy for that."

"He may have picked up some stupid ideas in that direction too. They are all the same, Essenes and New Alliance and followers of the Baptist. Indeed, all the heretics. Instead of regarding women as in their nature unclean, but necessary and even pleasant and sometimes praiseworthy, they have this idea that women may be in some spiritual respects the same as men. Then they see that this is not so and rush into another extreme. They end by being afraid of them and refusing even to touch them. It is so with many of their ideas, which may have a sound basis but are always carried far beyond any sensible point." He shook his head.

11—BYK

"Will you try, after the Sabbath, to get hold of young John for me? I must do my best to have a sensible talk with him."

"I'll see what I can do," said Caiaphas, "but I have no idea at all where he might be."

.   .   .   .   .

In fact, John had gone over to Joseph of Arimathæa's town house. He had stayed for a while in the Ophel, but the little room seemed to stifle him, and his hopeless pity for the poor girl who had been broken by what she had seen. There were practical decisions to make about the body, and Joseph was very helpful. It should, they thought, go back into Galilee for permanent burial. Later on, something could be built, some memorial or place for teaching.

All the time John kept remembering things said which might have started the idea of some other ending. But not now. He remembered a picture he used to make of how one day his Master would disappear, into the desert or over the edge of some tremendous height, higher than Tabor. And after they had lamented him, he would come back in glory. Three days afterwards; yes, he had said three days. But John would have known somehow, through his lamentation, that the other thing was going to happen, he would have been prepared for it. Now, having seen the body, the blue raised bruises with the skin tight or grazed and broken over them, the bitten lips, the slightly squinting, cold eyes, the horribly torn hands and feet, the deadness of the dead, he could not hope for anything.

"You were close to him, John," said the older man; "what did he intend when he came to Jerusalem?"

"He wanted to show us some essential aspect of the Kingdom," said John, "something that would explain and prove everything. But there is no explanation for what has actually happened—I mean, no explanation that makes sense of it in terms of the Kingdom, the new way."

"Only that the world will not accept him or it. Possibly

that is always so. We think that we, at least, if we had lived
in the old days, would have recognised the prophets for what
they were. But perhaps not, John, perhaps not."

His wife brought in sweetmeats, silent, her head tightly
shawled; they ate them, a little absent-mindedly. It was
difficult to make the kind of return to ordinary life which
seemed to be called for, but which John could not, so far,
accept. He could see nothing ahead of him, although he was
beginning to think that he must try to continue the teaching
of his Master and friend. He was not a good public speaker;
perhaps he could write some of it down or talk to a few
people at a time. But it could never be the same. "He told
me," said John, "that after he was gone—but somehow we
never believed that the time would come—there would be a
spirit that would come to us and help us. Perhaps it is too
soon to think of that."

"He spoke of joy, too, I think you told me, following the
grief. I cannot see how that will ever be, at any rate for you
and the rest who loved him so much. It might be that, as
others begin to follow his teachings . . . But could this be?
John: if he was Messiah, how can his teaching help us
without him? How can the Kingdom come when the King
is taken and destroyed by the enemy?"

John said slowly: "There was a thing that his brother
James said. For a moment it made me think. . . . But the
Essenes see things differently, and perhaps the words meant
something else. They have another kind of law."

"The New Alliance goes on although the Master of
Righteousness was killed bearing witness to their Way. Yet
there are so few of them. Just a small community barely
existing up there in the dry, salt hills, some distance off the
Jericho road. Seldom seen." He shook his head.

"What was their Master of Righteousness like? Do you
know?"

"He followed the way of mercy and brotherhood and the
relinquishing of all possessions, whether in goods and land

or, so to speak, in the family. All ties were to be cut. He was of an utterly pure life, or so it is said. He did not believe in taking up the sword against his enemies, but trusted in heaven and the justice of the Lord. And his enemies killed him. Yes, they killed him too. John, my son, the world is darkened for me, thinking of all these things." He stood up. "These poor Galileans. We must do what we can to help them. I suppose they will go back to the fishing."

"Rocky has a wife and a couple of little boys, I think. He just left them when the call came. His father will have taken care of them. Village folk are kindly. I suppose he will go back and live out the rest of his life at the fishing, and the memory of all this will begin to fade."

"And his mother?"

"I have—a special duty towards her. But perhaps she will want to go back with Simon. She was always a woman who knew what she wanted to do and be. Then, there are our friends in Bethany. When I think that he raised Lazarus from the dead!"

"But for himself he could do nothing."

"I know—I know," said John violently, "that if he had wanted to, he could have saved himself. Why would he not do it? That is the riddle he has set us. I think he might have come clear of the whole thing at any time—yes, even on the cross, if he had chosen!"

"You really think that?" Joseph said, frowning.

"I do think so. I believe he was tempted to save himself. And refused. But why—why—did he accept all this—this human suffering? Why did he accept death? I have to know. Oh, I have to know!"

Twenty-One

IN the guardroom, the soldiers were discussing the day, desultorily. The only interesting thing was that one of the men had at last had a success in the family where he used to go on occasional evenings off. It had taken a good while to get round them, but a man loses his taste for the casual satisfaction in a doorway or even in a hired bed; cheap goods, not too clean. This had been so long in coming to the point that he'd often felt like taking it by force and be hanged to the consequences. Still, it had been worth the wait, and his description of his juicy little peach fairly made the others' mouths water.

Two of them had been on guard duty at the last crucifixion. Look, that was a nice bit of stuff, good pure linen; they'd taken it off that chap that had called himself King. "I bet it was one of the girl friends wove it for him," the man said. "There were the devil of a lot standing around and howling."

"There were quite a few men," said the other. "Oh, I had my eyes skinned. I wonder if they'll make trouble? You never know, with these natives."

"They can be mopped up," said the other. "No bother! And if we don't do it, I know who will—that Sadducee lot. Hates them like poison, to my way of thinking." He took another handful of sunflower seeds and began to crack them, methodically.

"A funny crowd, these Jews," said the first; "always doing something queer. Getting worked up about it."

"What I can't stick is the way they kind of look down on

us. In spite of us being the occupying power. That gives me the creeps."

"You get the same with the Germans," a man said from across the room, tossing his olive stones into the fire, "stalking around thinking they're something superior. And they're only a lot of savages. The Jews are civilised, anyway. Look at their houses and this Temple of theirs all covered with marble and gold. And the shops in the goldsmiths' street! There's a lot of money around."

"Yes. It wouldn't be half bad if they'd give us the word to let loose in Jerusalem!" They all laughed; it was a constant thought.

"This Jew who called himself King," said the man from the crucifixion party, "I suppose that was the same thing. Getting it into his head he was something above everyone else."

"Ah. He had it coming to him." He looked across to the doorway; someone coming in a hurry: "Ah, young Marcus! What's up? Someone been saying something about Bulls?"

Marcus didn't even answer that one. He said: "This chap that's been crucified—who was he?"

"What—this King one?"

"I've been hearing stories about him . . ."

"You don't want to go believing what the natives say, son," said one of the older men, kindly enough.

". . . about his being someone separate from the rest of us, not fathered by man, born strangely, about his blood . . ."

The man who had won the piece of linen folded it up and came over. "Marcus," he said, "you've been letting one lot of words meet up with another lot you've got in your head. Always coming out with them, aren't you? Blood and cleansing and sin and that. If you'd been on duty you'd have seen this chap suffering and dying like the next. Nothing special about him, see?"

Marcus sat down on the step. "You're sure? You saw him die? He—just died?"

"Of course."

"Well—if that's all there is to it. Funny. I thought for a moment . . ."

"You let yourself get all worked up, young Marcus. What you need is a nice girl. No, no, don't start the whole thing all over again! I know you've got your reasons." He patted the young soldier on the back. Marcus looked a bit sick, sitting there, letting on he was polishing his helmet. He'd have had an excuse to feel sick if he'd been on crucifixion duty, not being used to it. But it was only the spring going to his head and no sensible way to give it a let-out. Besides—all these religions hotted it up round this time of year. Probably the lad had been off at his cave or whatever he called it, going through the motions and getting all worked up. On top of that he hears something about this Galilean that ties on. And what with the storm and the earthquake and the nasty feel of Jerusalem with all the pilgrims, you can't wonder if a chap gets upset. Better give him something to do. "We'll need some more firewood," he said; "it's over at the far gate. Take a couple of auxiliaries and get us some in, will you?"

Marcus got up, a little unsteadily, then straightened up, put on his helmet, walked outside and snapped out an order.

.   .   .   .   .

It was beginning to get cold again; nice enough after a warm day, but the storm had been chilly, apart from the gusts of hot dust. You needed some kind of warmth in the house. There were plenty of charcoal braziers in the Residence, which slaves carried from room to room, so that their masters and mistresses should always be warm. Many of these dated from the old Herod's time, and were elaborate affairs in bronze or brass or silver with patterns of vines and pomegranates and twisted handles. The whole place was equally elaborate, the walls slabbed with coloured marbles, the doorways sheathed with bronze, torch holders made like flowers or lions, chairs and couches ramping into griffins and chimeras. Lady Claudia had enjoyed it at first. Now she was not so sure. She wondered if her husband really intended to go home later in the year.

Lights, as well as warmth, preceded her. She settled herself on a couch, Barsiné laid a warm shawl over her knees, and the supper tray was brought in by the other maids: lambs' tongues, a salad, bread with cream cheese and a thick fish sauce, imported of course. There was some dried fruit and a sweet Greek wine which she watered well. There was always ice, or rather impacted snow, brought down from the Lebanon wrapped in layers of blanket and hurried along by night when it was cooler. Such things were her due. Occasionally she would ask Gaius Crispus's wife to come and have supper with her, but tonight that particular chatter was the last thing she wanted.

Suddenly she remembered the singing in the morning, and asked Barsiné if the Adonis mourners had come home. "Yes," said Barsiné, "they were frightened of the storm. They said it would bring bad luck; perhaps Adonis would not rise."

"They say he will come to life again, do they?"

"Yes," said Barsiné, "he was killed by something *she* sent . . ."

"Who? Is it the Aphrodite of these parts?"

"Yes. His lady. The one that loves him. She kills him so that he will live again, and be young for her. New and new he comes. That is what the mourners say."

"It is a kind of Mystery," said Claudia, "but only the common people go mourning, I suppose?"

"Only the women," said Barsiné; "men do not understand."

Claudia finished the raisins; she felt very restless, longed for something she could really pay attention to. One of the slaves, a cheerful little black girl, brought in the perch of parakeets. Claudia fed them with nuts, but one of them pecked at her and she sent the stupid creatures away. No, she didn't want to read, nor to have music; she couldn't think of any game she wanted to play. At last she said: "Have I anything fit to wear in Rome? If I haven't I must get something woven. I'd better look over my dresses, Barsiné."

Barsiné was delighted. It was an important feeling, taking out the dresses, which were for the most part long pieces of variously decorated material, which would be gathered at the shoulder, when worn, and becomingly tied at the waist, or emphasising the breasts, so that the pleats fell evenly. Some had embroidered belts, but others were meant to be worn with gold or silver links. Barsiné ordered the other slave girls about, held up the dresses, pointed out tiny holes and weak places. She hoped her lady would order the head of the weavers' guild to come over to the Residence. Then there would be a great considering of samples, matching of colours, and so forth. Some of the old dresses would come her way, and she in turn would hand down something nearly worn out to one of the new little slaves, who would kiss her hands. But that wasn't really what counted. The great thing was that her mistress and she were doing something together and her mistress was coming out of the mood—the bewitchment—whatever it was that had been on her.

They were in the middle of this when word came that Madame Joanna, the wife of Chuza, was there and had asked if she might see the Lady Claudia. For a moment Claudia hesitated, and Barsiné hoped with all her heart she wouldn't receive this one who had left her so sad and worried the last time. But in the end she said yes, she would see Madame Joanna. Barsiné was to put the dresses away; tomorrow would be time enough. And she was to remember to keep out the silver-shot blue to look at by daylight; she was sure it was beginning to tarnish.

Madame Joanna came in. She had obviously come straight from home and from the Passover feast, for she was

very magnificently dressed, though with an elaboration
which Claudia found in rather strange taste. There was some
kind of woman attendant with her, carrying a lamp, a slave
perhaps, in a dark shapeless cloak, who stood at the door and
said nothing to anyone. Madame Joanna began at once:
"We heard that His Excellency did his best to save him. I am
sure we have to thank you for that, and this is the message I
am bringing, and not from myself alone. From others, to
you. But the enemy was too strong, too cunning. You will
know that, Lady Claudia. You will also know that he is
—dead. With all his powers that might have been used. All
his love."

"I am—sorry," said Claudia inadequately, and then: "I
had always hoped to see him."

"Now it is too late. But we, who have understood his
teaching, must go on as far as we can. He gave us a special
kind of knowledge; we must try to apply it, hoping we shall
do so as though he were still with us." Madame Joanna was
speaking quietly, without violence. If she had wept, that was
all over.

"There was something you were saying this morning,"
Claudia said, "about all people being the children of God.
All people. It occurred to me, on thinking it over, that this
was scarcely—well, scarcely an idea that is usual in this
country. But perhaps I am wrong."

Joanna even smiled a little. "It is not the only one of his
thoughts that is a step forward from the old law that we, the
Jewish people, have honoured. It is a step forward, also,
from the Temple that keeps you at arm's-length in the outer
court, on pain of death, and me almost at arm's-length in the
next court because I was born a woman. It interests you,
Lady Claudia?"

"And all kinds of life, you said, were in relation to God.
Not only people. Birds and beasts and trees and all natural
things."

"Yes. The question is, how can we show our brotherhood

towards all this family? It should be easy, but everything makes it difficult, everything that we call——"

"Civilisation," said Claudia dryly. It was all making her a little uncomfortable. And yet she wanted to know more. There was something about it that corresponded to a need she had. It would be—better than the Mysteries. If once she could see it. And yet it was all to do with a Jewish peasant whom her husband had condemned—perhaps reluctantly— to death. Was she being disloyal to her husband and to the Roman Government and power to think of a condemned criminal as having some meaning or message for herself? Suddenly she wished her husband would come back and strengthen her in being a Roman.

"Yes," said Madame Joanna, "it will be very difficult. Yet I believe he showed us a way and a relationship with God." For a moment she said nothing, nor was there anything Claudia felt she could say in return; nothing seemed quite to fit. Then Barsiné came tiptoeing over and held something out to Madame Joanna. It was the bracelet she had thrown down earlier in the day. Absently Madame Joanna held out her wrist; Barsiné slipped it over and stepped back quickly, her breath short in her throat; now the thing would be away, out of the house with any bewitchment it might have brought with it! Madame Joanna rose: "Lady Claudia, I came to give you that message. And now I must go on. To others. No, I thank you, but I will not eat now. Should you ever want to see me again, I am at your service." She touched her hands to her forehead and heart, quickly, but with dignity. And then she went out, followed by the shadowy servant. Lady Claudia stayed, not moving from her couch; she had a walnut between her fingers and she rubbed it slowly into dry crumbs.

Then suddenly Barsiné ran over and knelt in front of her: "Do not see her again, my lady, do not see her! She will bewitch you, the same as that man did! Oh, do not let yourself be bewitched!"

It was odd. She almost felt that Barsiné was right. If only her husband would come back. But there, when he did he would probably be unwilling to talk to her at all, to give her any assurance. He might be drunk. He had probably spent the evening with one of those revolting girls. She herself had once, for a short time, had a lover. It was the fashionable thing. But she had not really enjoyed the experience, whereas he seemed almost to need this succession of little wretches to keep him in a good humour. And she must pretend not to notice or care. Perhaps when he got her message he would just laugh; he would make some excuse and wouldn't even see her. She felt oddly desolate, looking over Barsiné's head at the blurring candles. But all the same, she hoped her husband would come back from the Antonia soon.

Twenty-Two

(*9 to 10 p.m.*)

"I'M going out a minute," said Stormy. His brother followed him. They couldn't stand being in the same room as poor Miss Mary. Rocky could see that. And it was their mother who had said to him he'd better try to heal her. As though he had it in him to do that now. She could see he couldn't; that was why she was jibing at him, and because she was feeling bad herself. He didn't hold it against her. But all the same, the devils had been chased out of Miss Mary once, as he remembered very clearly: why not again?

He was alone in the room now; he couldn't any longer distract himself by talking to Stormy about the fishing. What was it that used to happen when the Son healed people? Where had he got the strength to pull them back into life and balance? He thought of the boy at Nain; they had all been there and seen the bier carried out and heard the poor woman lamenting. Why had the Son suddenly felt strength coming to him so that he could speak to the boy, command the return of the soul, the starting up of the heart, the breath coming back through the lips? And Jair's daughter; he had been in the darkened room with the dead girl on the bed with the embroidered hangings, white and dead and lovely, a young, young lass. And she too had answered to the command.

And he himself—yes, he had done healing and teaching, but always with the knowledge of who was behind him. And I couldn't always manage it, he thought; I didn't have enough faith. I'd start out to do a thing, certain it would be

easy, and then it wouldn't be easy and I'd make some kind
of slip and then all my faith would be away in a minute like
water out of a sieve. He'd be angry with me for not having
more faith, and the very minute I felt him angry, felt the
fire of his love and anger on me, then I'd be all right again.
And it was me that first said who he was, when the others
were thinking it, right enough, but not quite daring to say
it. I out and said it aloud. I said he was the Son. And me
saying it—that did something for him; I suppose, in a way of
speaking, it strengthened *his* faith.

But now I don't think I can do anything. It seems as if I'm
cut off from the spring. I can't go back to him and say, what
did I do wrong? And he won't ever any more come and tell
me off, saying to me: Rocky, can't you understand what I
mean? He'd stand over me half angry and half laughing,
and I'd try to understand, though it was harder than
maybe he thought, but then, all of a sudden, I'd find
myself understanding as clear as—as water on a summer
day when you put your head under and open your eyes
and look.

All right. I'll try to understand now. And if I can once
get round to understanding, then I'll know in myself that I
can help Miss Mary. Dear friend, dear Master, although
you're dead, help me. Help your Rocky.

Flash opened the door from the street a crack. He didn't
want to come back in if Miss Mary was screaming, or just
going to scream. But it wasn't her he saw at the first glance.
He stepped back cautiously and shut the door so that it made
no sound. "Stormy," he said, "do you know what's
happening? Rocky's praying in there. And do you know
what it makes me think of? It makes me think of *him* the way
he was over at Gethsemane. Let's go away, shall we?"

"There's not going to be anything happening to Rocky, is
there?" said his brother, "not—not something laid on him?
I wouldn't want it, Flash; no, I wouldn't!"

Flash looked at his brother. "No," he said, "it's not that.

But I was thinking. Maybe that's what we should be doing ourselves."

.   .   .   .   .

The moon was high now, white and round and cold, putting out the stars nearest to it, making a roof here and there shine as though it had been raining. Those were the same stars they steered their boats by at the night fishing, the very same stars away down here in Jerusalem. They stood and watched them. The things they were turning over in their minds were too difficult to say aloud. They heard steps in the distance. After a while Stormy said: "It's John Priest." And so it was. He had not been able to stay quietly anywhere. He had been from Joseph's house to the garden, but had heard Salome and some of the other women talking and had come away again. Now he felt he must go back to the Ophel and see how things were there.

"No," said Stormy. "When we left, Miss Mary was the same, but Rocky is praying. And perhaps he'll get strength. You see, John, there was a time when we were all sent out and given power to teach and heal. We were like kings. He made us like kings. You know, we went out just as we were, without any money or even a change of clothes. And wherever we went people knew who we'd come from, and mostly we were welcome. I don't remember ever going hungry. And all the time we were sailing along on this wave of certainty he'd sent us out with. We knew we could do whatever he'd told us to do. Then we'd come back and tell him how things had gone. That was a good year, wasn't it, Flash? If only it could have gone on."

John said: "He was using you as extra hands, as bits of himself. Was that how you felt?"

"That was it," said Stormy; "yes, that was it, right enough. We could all do it. We'd only to think of him and it was easy. But, you see, John, it wasn't ever ourselves. We knew that. Although we were kings we weren't proud. He'd have known if we had been. And if we'd ever thought it was our own doing, then we wouldn't have been able. Sometimes we did, all the same, and then nothing worked. We couldn't find the words for our teaching; we couldn't heal." He looked at Flash; they both seemed to remember some particular occasion, and laughed.

"I wish I'd been with you then!" said John.

"I wish you had too. There was Mat who used to be a tax collector up Capernaum way, and some people wondered that he could do it, for he'd never been one for prayer and fasting. But then, nor had we. And we'd all sinned plenty. We didn't know there was any other way, not when we were lads. But that was forgiven and we could start out new with him guiding us all the time. And now we're wondering . . ."

"What?"

"Well, oughtn't we, maybe, to try, in spite of him not being there any longer—and he said, he always said he wouldn't be with us for ever, but we couldn't believe it, could we, Flash?"

"No," said Flash; "he told us, in a way, everything that was going to happen, but we didn't think he meant it, not as something in the real world. . . ."

They were all three walking back towards the little house; there was hardly anybody about. It was only the most urgent business that would take anyone out on the night of the Sabbath which had also been Passover for many. In the darkness all the words he had ever spoken came back round them, needing to be made clear. Suddenly John said: "You will remember certain things he said about—coming back."

"I remember them well," said Stormy, "but you see, John, he was always speaking in stories and pictures. Maybe he meant that he would come back into our minds so strong that we'd be given strength too, like we had that year. If he does come back, it won't be himself, the one we knew. It will be someone like—like God." Neither of the other two answered. He went on with what was in his mind. "Whether

or not, I believe we shall have to try to be like we were
then."

"You are braver than I am," John said, and suddenly
found himself being, yes, jealous of the fishermen who had
managed to grasp this solid and terrible thing, this hope out
of despair. He took the jealousy out and tried to look at it as
the evil thing it was. But for a while he could not answer
Stormy as he wanted to, with love.

They were at the door now and Stormy was putting out
his hand to open it, but Flash caught hold of him. "Listen!"
he said. They all stood quite still and listened and looked at
one another. It was Rocky's voice they heard. Yet in a way
it wasn't. It had his accent and intonation, but something
had happened to it. It was speaking with that authority and
certainty which they used to know, from one only. It was
speaking to Mary. It was commanding her in the name of
Jesus of Nazareth and through his power and his love which
she knew. It was drawing her out of the inner world of night
and terror and cutting violent colours into the outer world
of morning and acceptance. They could hear her voice
replying, very faintly, and it was the voice of the Mary who
had been with them all these months, ever since the day she
had left her father's house in Magdala. Then it was Rocky
speaking again. And then Mary's voice, strengthening and
filling out; she said: "They are gone. Dear Rocky. Dear
friend. They are all gone. I am back in the world he showed
me!"

Stormy turned to the other two, his hand still on the door.
In the clear moonlight, John could see it, a broad, strong
hand with short nails, a hand that had never held a pen, the
hand of a fisherman, a man fisher. Stormy said: "You see—
don't you? That's what I meant. He's come back to Rocky
and, just the same, he's going to come back to all of us!"

Yes, thought John, yes, I do see. And I see myself small
and naked like a worm. He caught hold of Stormy. "Forgive
me!" he said.

12—BYK

"What for?" said Stormy, and then, slowly: "You doubted, John. But so did I. So did Flash. And the others doubted so much it made them cowards. And they don't know yet; they'll be doubting still and they'll be miserable like we were five minutes ago. Do you remember, John, how unhappy we were? I can only just remember!" But he's dead, thought John, he's dead. And then: Stormy never saw him dead. Not with his own eyes. I did. That unhappiness hasn't changed.

Stormy was looking at him hard, saw the tears on his face in the moonlight. "John," he said, "I don't mean I'm not unhappy. But I'm happy too."

"Yes," said John, "perhaps that's what was meant. You've understood it."

Stormy looked at his brother, then he said: "Me and Flash, there were times we've said to one another: John Priest, he's different, he can't be one of ourselves, he's bound to look down on us. And now I know I was wrong. I know we're together now, for always. Let's go in now, shall we, John? I—I want to see them both."

"So do I!" said John.

Twenty-Three

GAIUS CRISPUS accompanied the Procurator back from the Antonia to the Residence; he had his own separate suite there. There was, of course, a guard, and Hector following behind, feeling rather tired and with a nagging headache about which he could grumble to no one. The guards sang as they marched, at first in low voices, but after His Excellency joined in, with gusto and the pleasant feeling that it would impress the natives who were skulking in their houses as they always did on the Sabbath. When they got to the door, Barsiné pulled Hector to one side, roughly, so that he shouldn't get ideas, and gave him the message from her mistress. He transmitted it to His Excellency, who seemed rather taken aback. "What does she want?" he asked. Gaius shook his head and withdrew slightly. He could imagine Lady Claudia wanting many things and not getting them. The Procurator went on, half to himself: "I suppose she's heard about my little piece over at the Antonia. My virtuous Claudia doing her duty as a good wife and all that. Well, it can't be helped. I'll sell the other one tomorrow if it makes for a quiet life. She's not up to some I've had, anyway; gets all worked up if you want her to—oh well. Not worth a row with Claudia. I might marry the girl off. Hector might like her, what?"

Hector smiled deprecatingly. He didn't suppose H.E. was serious, but if he was . . . For a moment his headache disappeared entirely.

"What does your mistress want, eh?" the Procurator asked Barsiné. But Barsiné shook her head; she was much too scared to answer. "Pretty little thing," he said to Gaius in Latin, which the girl wouldn't understand. "I wonder if there'd be anything doing?"

"Better not, sir!" said Gaius hurriedly. That would be a row and no mistake.

"I suppose I'd better see her," His Excellency said, "though I can't say the prospect is very appealing. However . . . No, Gaius, I'm not letting you off. Your wife'll be asleep. Anyhow you can't want her, not after . . . Just stay here. All right, Barsiné, tell your mistress that I shall be honoured if she will have the goodness to come and see me. And get in something to eat, Hector! And drink."

He turned along the side of the courtyard. There were myrtles in tubs and pomegranates in early leaf that showed prettily in the moonlight. There was a bed of lilies, too, pouring out scent into the night. His own little room was plain enough; the Herodian decoration had been painted over. There had been too many of these pomegranates and stars, something to do with native magicians and kings, David and Solomon or some such names, and other people's magic was always something to be avoided. His Excellency sat down on a couch and threw his legs up, scowling at Gaius, who would have liked to go to bed. He was feeling soberer every minute. After a few moments Claudia came in; she was wearing quite an appetising dress, her husband noticed; funny, they used to get on quite well before she got so damned particular. Barsiné came after her, carrying a wrap. A few formal remarks were exchanged.

"You wanted to see me about something special, my lady?" Pontius Pilate said after a time: he was hoping to get it over. Gaius looked away, not wanting to get involved.

"Yes," she said nervously, and then: "I was wondering whether a message I sent to you this morning was delivered and if so whether—whether . . ."

"Yes, by Jove, it did," said her husband, remarkably

relieved. "And very sensible too. Very sensible indeed. I quite agreed with you, my dear. The man was as innocent as a child, and likeable too. I'd have let him off if I could possibly have managed it—and your message would have decided me. . . ." Gods, she was looking pleased!—and it suited her. "Yes, you were quite right, but the fellow was formally accused of *maiestas*—you know what I mean, my dear; something that takes away from the divinity, so to speak, of the Divine Emperor. Well, I had to take that seriously and, well, as a matter of fact, there were some threats from the Sadducee party—you remember, these fellows who are supposed to be our friends. I've an idea they had a special down on this man and had worked things out so that I had no alternative, no, I'm afraid that was clear, no alternative at all. However, you'll be pleased to hear that he died quite quickly and that some of his friends took him away and buried him decently."

"I am so glad you let them do that," said Claudia, and dabbed at her eyes. After all, there was nothing like the Roman way of doing things. Hector brought in a tray with some little cakes and the wine in silver cups. Her husband got up and served her himself.

"Yes, yes," he said, "I like to be merciful when possible, and someone seems to have put the body into his family vault for some reason; so it didn't end up too badly. It wasn't such a win for the Sadducees as they think, either. I've used it to get the other party on my side, haven't I, Gaius?"

"Very neatly indeed, sir. So, whatever these peculiar people of Judæa decide later on—and they may well regret today's action—you will be in a good position. In fact, one way and another, I think one can say you will have increased your popularity."

"If I've managed to put a spoke in the wheel of this Caiaphas and his friends, I'll be happy," the Procurator said. "He thinks he can run this place as a kind of theocracy.

What's more, when they stop wanting to be so Jewish—and I don't blame them for that—they all go Greek. Talk about Athens. Not Rome. Dirty little Athens!" He grinned at Hector, who had been hurt by this, and had also realised that things being as they were, it was no use expecting the reversion of H.E.'s popsy. His headache was getting worse.

"It does seem a shame, though," Lady Claudia said. "But I'm so grateful that you did your best and that my little note was not in any way—well, something I ought not to have sent."

"Not a bit, my lady," said the Procurator heartily; "but what was it made you take an interest in the man?"

"Well," she said, "there were things I heard. I saw him once. And actually I had hoped to meet him. And then Madame Joanna, the wife of Chuza, you know, told me all about him. Such a nice sensible woman; one could really make friends with her. She told me so many interesting things. I feel I am beginning to understand the Jews a little better."

"Are you, by Jove! Well, you'll have to explain them to me; I find them devilish difficult."

"Perhaps they find you difficult too."

Pontius Pilate bellowed with laughter. "That's a good one! Isn't that a good one, Gaius? I'm sure I hope they do! But what did you think of that man—what was his name, Gaius?—oh, Jesus—Jesus son of Joseph. From Galilee somewhere. Tell me what you made of him, my lady. Was he a magician? Or what?" They had been talking in Latin and Barsiné hardly understood any of it, only that her lady was pleased and her lord was gracious. But here was a word she did know. She stiffened: the name and the word.

Claudia hesitated: "No, I do not think he was a magician. I think he was a good man, perhaps a mystic. He was familiar with the gods, or perhaps I should say with his God."

"That would be the God of the Jews here?"

"Yes, yes. But he had some new way of looking at this God. Or perhaps all gods; I'm not sure. Some way of thinking about people in relation to the purpose of the heavens. I'm putting it badly. But one always supposes that the gods are aspects of something beyond them that is too difficult to make into a picture."

"The Gods are in the hands of Necessity. The same as the rest of us," said her husband with a certain seriousness; it was one of the few things he believed. "They can't dodge it. Beyond a point. With magic, you can dodge a bit. But this man didn't seem to be trying to."

"No. No, I doubt if that would have been how he would have put it to himself, even. But perhaps in a way he was a dangerous man. You will remember the original doctrine of Epicurus." She looked round. Gaius was frowning. For a brief moment Hector looked interested. She went on: "About the brotherhood of man, you know. I wonder how that doctrine would affect a State if anyone were to believe in it—sincerely?"

"I seem to remember a lot of things that old boy said," remarked the Procurator, "that had a lot more to them than brotherhood: for instance, about enjoying oneself. Seeing there is no punishment and no reward." Hector listened in annoyance at this Roman garbling of the Epicurean philosophy, but of course it was not his place to interrupt. Typical of them to take out just the bit that suited them and then blow it up into the main thing!

Claudia said: "But if everyone seriously believed in the brotherhood of man?"

"That would be crazy. If this fellow believed that, it's just as well he's dead."

"I think he did. At least in some kind of way. Oh—oh, my dear friend—is it wrong of me to be thinking so earnestly about a condemned criminal?"

"It's a bit odd, you know." His Excellency leaned over

and patted her on the shoulder. "But we can't have you crying like that. He does seem to have done something to you, my dear. Now, I'm going to tell you something. After it was all over I held a little private ceremony, just to avert any influences there might have been. I'm not saying there were. But supposing he was dedicated to this God and supposing he was unjustly condemned, even if I was anxious to avoid doing it—as I was—well, the God might be angry. Such things have been known. Or again, if he had been a magician, he might have thrown some sorcery back over his shoulder, so to speak, when he was being marched off. Well, I went through the ceremony in front of our own gods; you understand what I mean, my dear? Gaius very kindly took the part of family friend."

"An honour," Gaius muttered in the background.

"So it went without a hitch. And I thought specially of you. I particularly averted any influences from you. So it's bound to be all right soon, even if, well, you did feel a certain, well, interest." He took a deep breath. He had made quite a speech. There, she'd stopped crying. After all, she was his lawful wife and he couldn't have her getting bewitched. Or whatever it was.

"So perhaps," she said, "I needn't have taken it so seriously?"

"No, of course not, my dear."

"And yet it was serious."

"Serious for him, poor chap!" said her husband, and suppressed a laugh.

She stood up. "As to the ceremony," she said. "I thank you, my friend. It has lightened my heart."

Her husband took her hand; then suddenly kissed her on the forehead. "I'll come and tuck you up, my dear," he said. She went out, with a slightly heightened colour and a little smile. In the courtyard she stopped and broke off one of the hot scented lilies and looked at it deeply between her hands in the moonlight. Barsiné followed her, happy.

"Well, well," said the Procurator, "that went off all right. I think I'll sell my little piece at the Antonia. D'you want her, Gaius? A special price for you. No? She'll fetch something. Too good to give away, eh, Hector?" But Hector was almost too tired even to hate his master.

Twenty-Four

SALOME and the other women had tried to get Mary to go back; it was too much for her; she should get some sleep now; they would do the watching. But she had refused. She would go back at dawn, perhaps. "Many a night I watched over him," she said, "and never too wearied." She sat on the ground with her back to an olive tree, a great old trunk, lined and weather-beaten as was her own face. She was trying to think about her son, but everything came in the way, the whisperings of the other women, the cold, clear moonlight, the memories of his babyhood that kept catching at easy tears, above all his body as she had seen it, the hours of pain, and the calling on his God who had forsaken him.

The moon climbed and climbed, was high and hard, like a piece of silver that one might lose off a head-dress and look for all night. He had watched her once doing that; how she had worried till she found it, sweeping under everything in case it had rolled into a corner. He hadn't helped her to look for it, though she had asked him to. He had been trying to tell her about something. She hadn't attended. It seemed to her now that this had kept on happening. He was always trying to tell her, or someone else, but most people were too busy. Those fishermen had dropped everything and listened, but it meant their poor fathers had taken over, just at an age when a man thinks he can sit back and live a bit easy. Zebedee—he'd had to hire men to take the place of the boys. And Rocky's poor wife. They'd lost by it, and all through

178

listening. Yet all the same, all the same, if only she knew now what it was he had been trying to tell her!

She'd picked up a few olives before she left the house and put them into a fold of her dress. She didn't remember taking them now, but there they were, little lumps. She began to eat them, slowly. She threw out the stones. One of the stones might grow, taking root among the rocks in the dry ground, and the sapling would come. But it would be thirty years before the olive would bear.

Salome came again, ducking under the branches, and offered her something to eat. The smell of the onions came at her strong and tasty. Yet it was nothing she wanted. She shook her head and murmured something.

"It's being too much for her," Salome said to one of the other women; "she ought to have taken my advice and gone home."

"And on the Sabbath too!" said her friend. "Oh, the cruelty of it!"

"We'll all be going home in the morning," Salome said, "and then we'll get some sense into her again."

"And to think of *him*, in behind that terrible stone," said another. "I used to listen to him. Yes, it did my heart good. You see, there I was, left a widow. I had two good sons, but one of them was killed by a block of marble falling on him; he was a quarrier. And the other went off to Africa or some terrible, far place, to make his fortune, and I never heard from him again. My daughter, she was married, but her husband used to beat her; she's dead too. So I had nothing left to live for till I heard tell about *him*." She rambled on, but nobody listened to her; misfortune was too common. He had listened, though.

Simon sat a little way off from the women. He felt out of place. That was how he often felt. But he had to stand by them, hadn't he? He thought about a couple of locked chests he had promised to make for a customer. He was a spice merchant. Very particular about the measurements and

the finish. He had gone down himself to the shop and
measured up. Would Jude be able to manage? He wasn't
much of a craftsman, hadn't been so long with their father.
He'd be upset when he heard about this.

Somebody else came into the garden. It was Madame
Joanna, whom they all knew, or knew about. She had two
servants with her, one of whom had a basket, which she took
round to the watchers. It had good stuff in it, better than
anything they'd brought; there were slices of cold meat and
sauce to dip it in. The widow didn't often get meat; timidly
she took a second piece, in her heart thanking him, who had
told Madame Joanna about the poor.

"Is Mary here?" Madame Joanna asked Salome, who
pointed to the dark shape under the olive tree. "Perhaps we
shouldn't disturb her," Madame Joanna said thoughtfully.
"She may be thinking that it was a wonderful thing to have
been his mother. She may be full of thanks and blessing."

But Salome thought that was a crazy thing to say. Rich
people were often crazy. One didn't contradict them, all
the same.

He would make a coffin, Simon thought suddenly, for his
brother. He'd use nothing but the best wood. Once they got
the body home to Nazareth, he'd do that before he laid a
finger on any other job. He thought out just the wood he
would use. It would take three days to get the body back,
along the Jordan road and then up, but it would have all
this stuff rubbed into it, so it would keep; that had all been
arranged. If only all the rich people were like this Joseph of
Arimathæa! He'd promised to help them over transport too.
And it was cool weather, anyhow, for the time of year.
Perhaps, even, his brother James might help. You never
knew if he would or wouldn't. He had his own reasons that
no ordinary person could understand. And then Simon
began to think how he had caught up with James on the
road out of Jerusalem and given him that message, and how
James had come back with him, and made that vow. He

began to wonder if he had heard it right; he hadn't been feeling up to much himself. What did it all mean?

Joanna and the other women were talking together in low voices. There were echoes of what *he* had said, their friend and teacher, in some of the things that Madame Joanna was saying, hurting and yet comforting, as though something were still going on, as though it could be built on. And it came into Salome's mind as a great surprise that it was like the old texts from the prophets; they seemed to grow all the time, as people turned them over and spoke about them. And these things Mary's boy had said, they were growing too. Under her nose almost. But that was with Madame Joanna being such a wise one. As wise as a man, almost.

In a while she asked them, where was Mary—young Mary from Magdala? Salome told about the devils coming back. She described it all, how the girl had gone a bit queer earlier that day after the rescue had failed, and then when it came to the un-nailing and hauling down of the body she just couldn't take it. She'd broken up, so to speak, and the devils had rushed in. So now she was back at the house in the Ophel and most likely she'd never be in her right wits again.

"You must bring her to me," said Madame Joanna. "I'll take care of her, poor thing. Perhaps—if I were to talk to her about *him* and bring him back into her mind . . ."

"It'll be no use," said Salome, shaking her head, "but if you'll take care of her I'm sure we shall all be ever so grateful. We'll have cares enough."

The door into the garden opened again; another voice. Under the ancient olive tree, Mary stirred. "Who is that speaking my name?" she said and stood up, and came out slowly, stooping under a heavy branch. "John, my son," she said and took his head in her hands and kissed it and pressed it against her breast. She said: "You have something to tell me. Something—good."

"Yes," he said, "how did you know—Mother?"

But she could not have answered that. It was like when the

words of a song came out of nowhere. "Tell me," she said. The others were gathering round, but at a little distance.

He said: "Mary of Magdala is well again. The devils are all cast out, just as they once were. Rocky did it. While we were all doubting and wondering, Rocky believed that your son's spirit would come to him in strength and would fill him so that he could heal her. And so it happened. As it came to Rocky, so it will come to all of us."

"Good news," said Mary, "good news indeed. And thanks to the Lord God of Israel who let me bear him and give him suck! For now his spirit has returned, and it is proof that he is the one I dreamt he was!" For a moment she stood upright like a young girl, a girl in her pride and beauty, carrying high on her head a pitcher of fresh water from the spring. Then she was little again and bent and clinging on to him.

Joanna said: "John, did you see this with your own eyes?" He nodded. "And Simon bar Jonas, did you see him truly filled with the spirit? As he was when Jesus sent him out, directly from himself, to heal and teach?"

"He was like that," said John; "astonished, and yet—full of certainty."

"Where were my boys?" said Salome. "Why did it have to be Rocky?"

"It will be the same for them," he said. "There is no greater or less in the Kingdom of Heaven."

"Do you mean—are they going to go about healing?"

"And teaching," said John, "there will be so much to do; for all of us, each in our way. I keep on thinking . . ."

"Running their heads into danger!" said Salome. "I thought that would be all over."

"Anything new is dangerous," said John uncertainly, wishing one of the women would speak to her.

It was Joanna who did: "It is dangerous to bear a child, Salome. But which one of us would not accept that danger? And when the man child is held up for us to see, which of us does not forget everything, in joy, yes, in joy!" And there was a kind of murmur of approval from the rest of the women.

"I would like my son James to know this," said Mary suddenly.

John hesitated, wondering if he should speak of the vow James had made. Simon touched him on the elbow. "Tell her," he said. "I can't." So John told her about the vow, and the others listened. To speak again with Jesus. Simon shook his head with a sick feeling. The spirit was one thing. But— to speak with him. Truly to speak. No, that would never speak, that bruised and broken body. The breath would never come back to it, the throat had closed up, the tongue and the lips that form the words, they were drying and hardening, already turning back to dust. And James would keep his vow.

That thought came to his mother too: "So I am to lose another of my sons," she said, and then, as though talking to herself: "I never loved him so much. Maybe that was why he went off and joined those strange ones, taking himself away from all of us. But he's my son. And stubborn. He will keep to it. And die."

"Can we be sure?" John said. "It was an answer to something which was said—a message for him . . ."

He could not finish his thought. It was too impossibly difficult. He found that Mary was looking at him intently, questioningly. There should be an answer. He did not know it yet. He looked instead at the great stone in front of the tomb that he had found so heavy. Joanna looked too, staring at it. Gradually they were all looking. The moonlight shone on it very coldly and distinctly, the stone between them and him.

Lightning Source UK Ltd.
Milton Keynes UK
19 February 2010

150351UK00001B/176/P